WELCOME TO
PASSPORT TO READING
A beginning reader's ticket to a brand-new world!

Every book in this program is designed to build read-along and read-alone skills, level by level, through engaging and enriching stories. As the reader turns each page, he or she will become more confident with new vocabulary, sight words, and comprehension.

These PASSPORT TO READING levels will help you choose the perfect book for every reader.

READING TOGETHER
Read short words in simple sentence structures together to begin a reader's journey.

READING OUT LOUD
Encourage developing readers to sound out words in more complex stories with simple vocabulary.

READING INDEPENDENTLY
Newly independent readers gain confidence reading more complex sentences with higher word counts.

READY TO READ MORE
Readers prepare for chapter books with fewer illustrations and longer paragraphs.

This book features sight words from the educator-supported Dolch Sight Words List. This encourages the reader to recognize commonly used vocabulary words, increasing reading speed and fluency.

For more information, please visit passporttoreadingbooks.com.

Enjoy the journey!

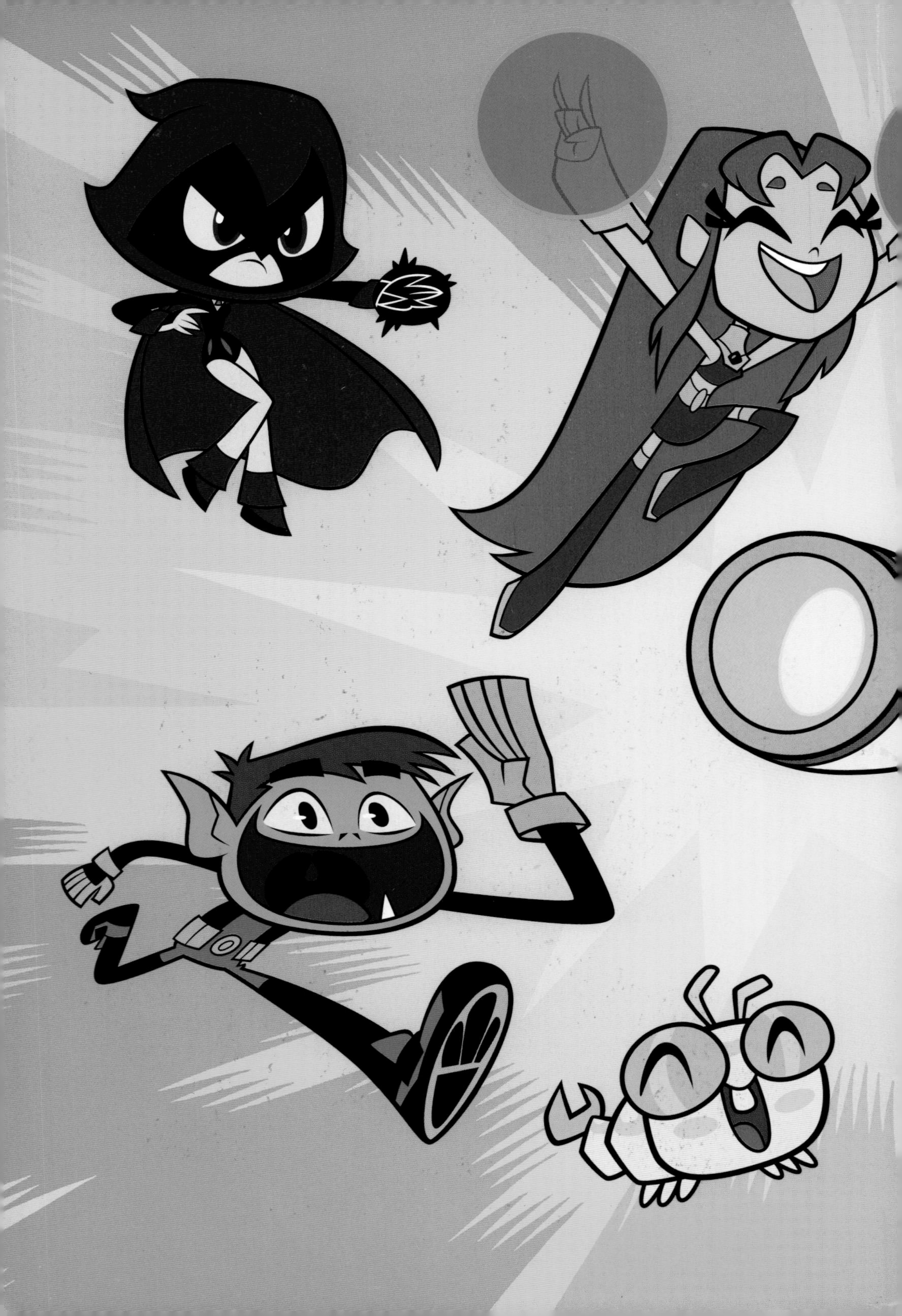

TEEN TITANS GO!

TEAM UP!

Ⓛ Ⓑ
LITTLE, BROWN AND COMPANY
New York   Boston

Meet the Teen Titans! originally published in 2014 by Little, Brown and Company
Boys Versus Girls originally published in 2015 by Little, Brown and Company
Brain Food originally published in 2015 by Little, Brown and Company
Tooth Fairy Freak-Out originally published in 2016 by Little, Brown and Company
Silkie Time originally published in 2017 by Little, Brown and Company
Pizza Power originally published in 2016 by Little, Brown and Company

Cover design by Carolyn Bull.

Little, Brown and Company
Hachette Book Group
1290 Avenue of the Americas, New York, NY 10104
Visit us at lb-kids.com

First Hardcover Edition: July 2017
First Paperback Edition: July 2017

Little, Brown and Company is a division of Hachette Book Group, Inc.
The Little, Brown name and logo are trademarks of Hachette Book Group, Inc.

The publisher is not responsible for websites (or their content)
that are not owned by the publisher.

ISBN 978-0-316-54857-1 (hc)—ISBN 978-0-316-54847-2 (pb)

Library of Congress Control Number: 2016954135

10 9 8 7 6 5 4

1010

Printed in China

The illustrations for this book were created digitally.
This book was edited by Russell Busse and designed by Carolyn Bull. The production
was supervised by Rebecca Westall, and the production editor was Jon Reitzel.
The text was set in Century Schoolbook, and the display type is Ed Interlock.

Passport to Reading titles are leveled by independent reviewers applying the standards
developed by Irene Fountas and Gay Su Pinnell in *Matching Books to Readers: Using Leveled Books
in Guided Reading*, Heinemann, 1999.

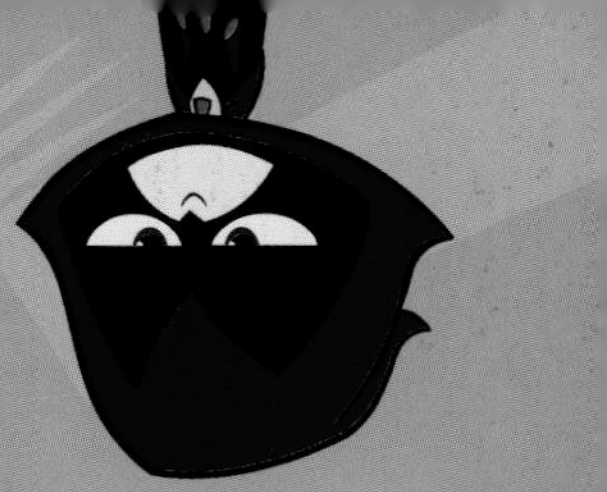

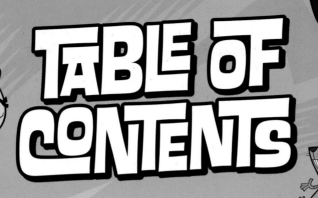

TABLE OF CONTENTS

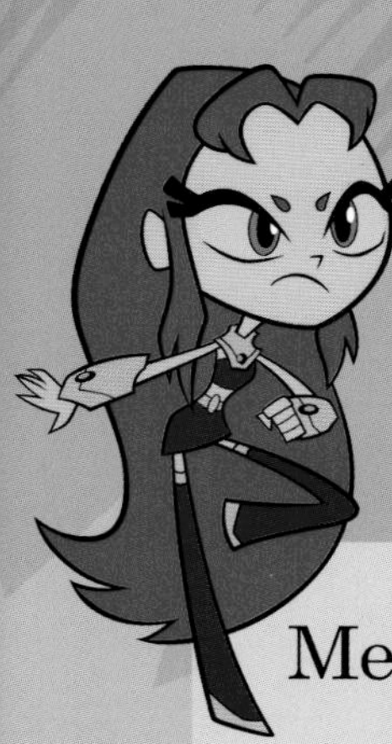

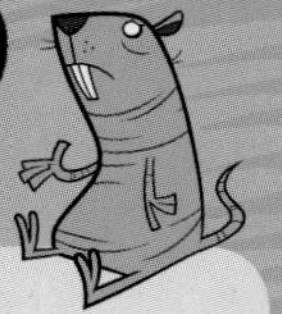

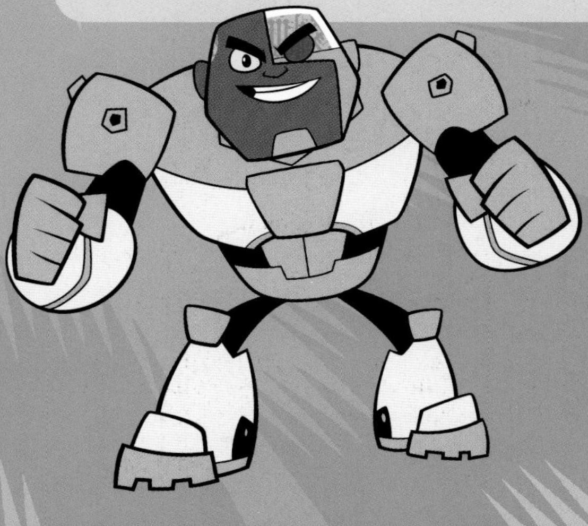

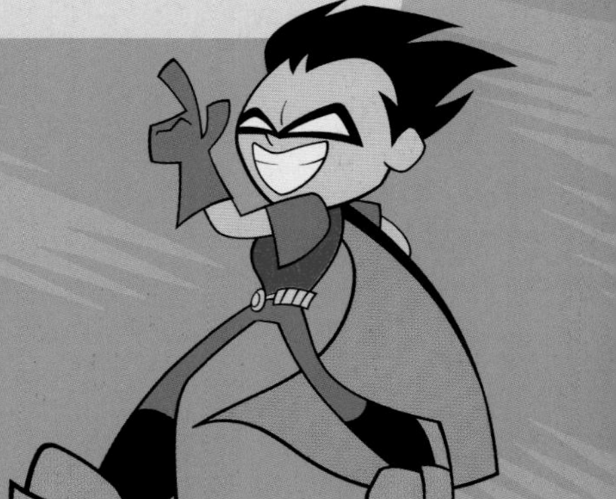

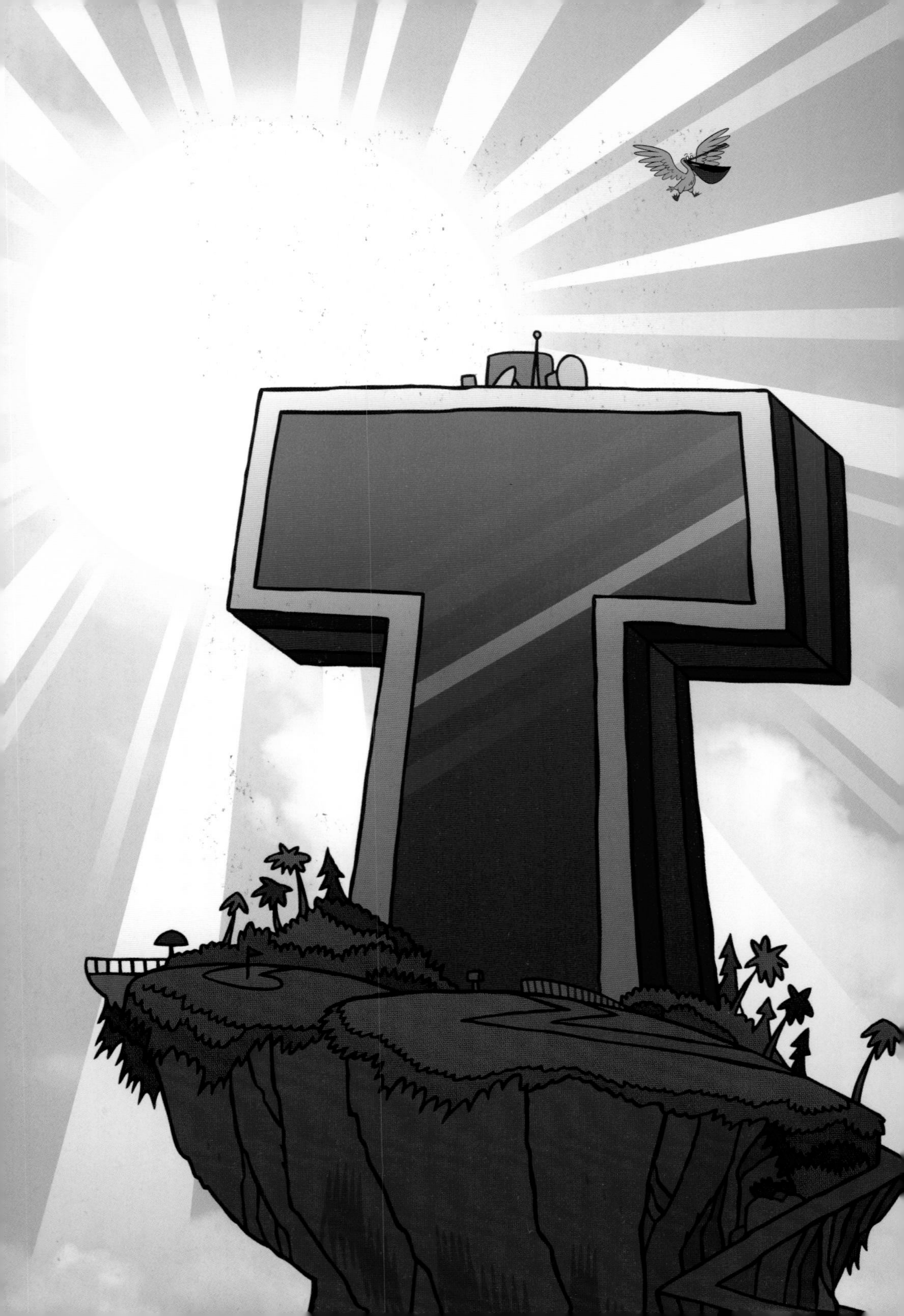

Adapted by Lucy Rosen
Based on the episode "Dude, Relax!"
written by Amy Wolfram

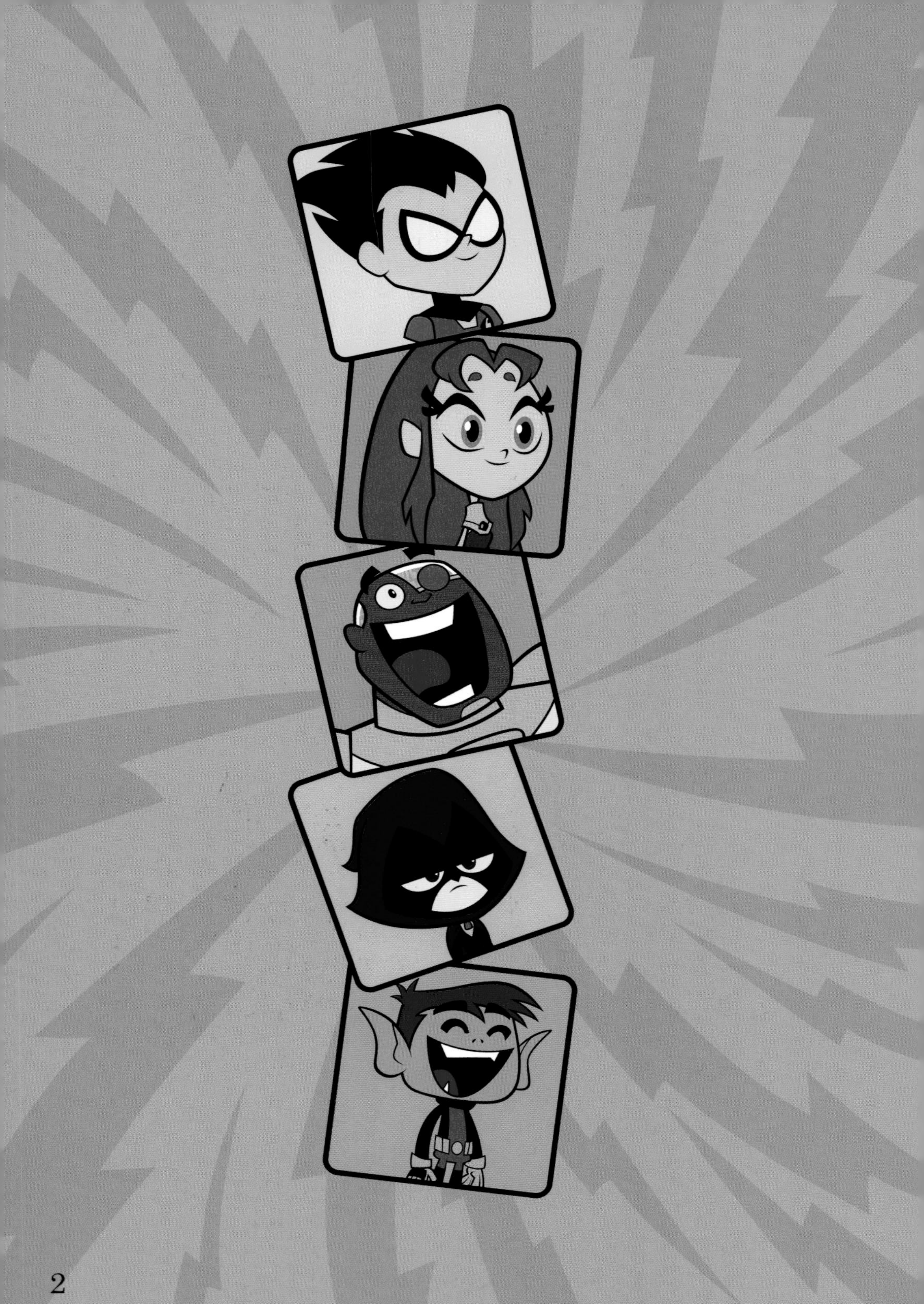

Attention, Teen Titans fans!
Look for these words when you read
this book. Can you spot them all?

insect

tool

couch

popcorn

The Teen Titans are an awesome bunch.

They combine their superpowers and become unstoppable!

Cyborg is half-man, half-robot.
He escapes danger
with his super-strength
and powerful armor.

Cyborg's robot parts are great tools.

His jet packs help him fly.
His arm cannons help him
blast through walls.

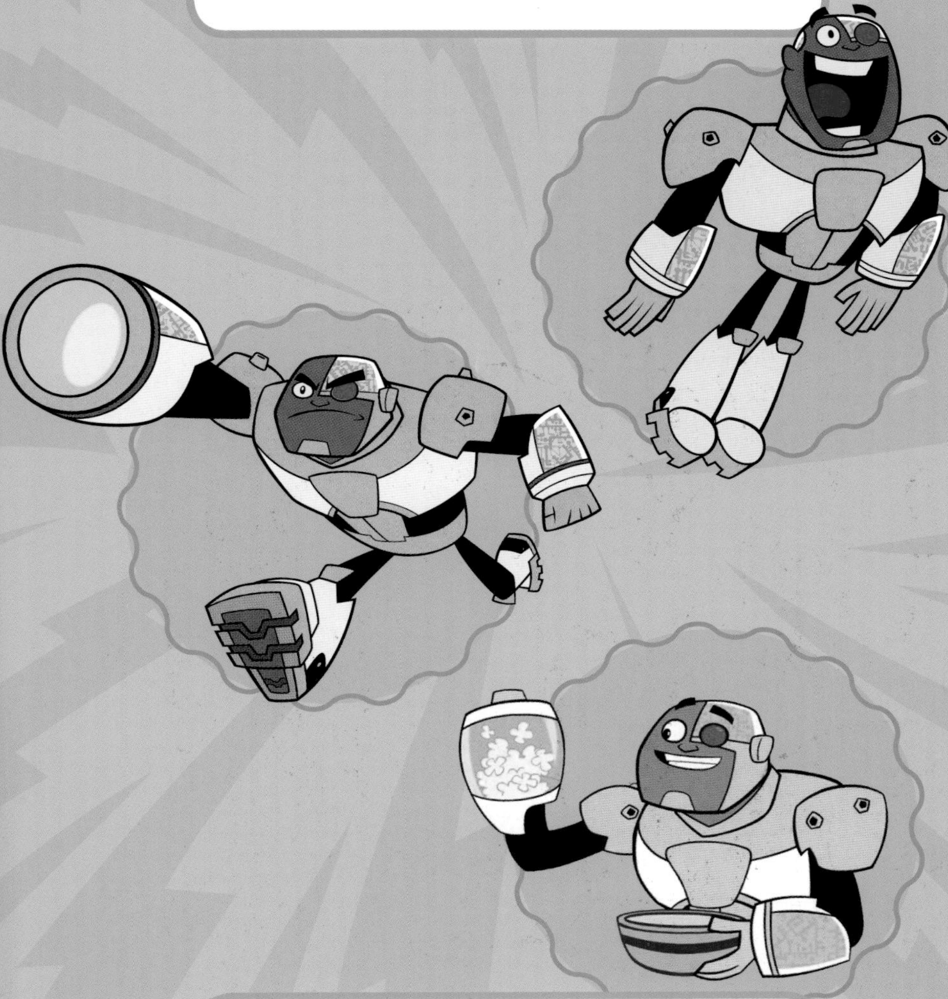

And when he gets hungry,
he can make snacks!

Beast Boy can change into any animal.
He can shrink down into an insect
or grow into a T. rex.

Whenever he changes shape,
he acts like a new critter.

Beast Boy has a silly side.
You never know what
he will turn into next!

Starfire can fly,
but she does not need a jet pack.
Starfire is an alien
from the planet Tamaran.

Starfire is kind and friendly,
but do not get her mad!
She shoots starbolts from her hands
and starblasts from her eyes.

Starfire has a pet named Silkie.
Silkie does not talk,
but he sure does eat...
anything but tofu.

Beast Boy likes Silkie's style.
He copies it sometimes!

Raven is the most serious of the group.
Her brain is her superpower.
She controls things with her mind
and casts powerful spells.

She can even transport herself
from place to place!

Robin is the Teen Titans'
fearless leader.

Robin is different
from the rest of the group.
He cannot fly or change shape.
He cannot move things with his mind.

Robin is a master detective,
an expert pilot,
and a very nimble acrobat.
His friends respect him.
His enemies fear him.

There is one thing that Robin
does not do well.
He does not know how to relax.

"We must always stay alert!" says Robin
as he scans his danger detector.
"Crime can happen at any moment!"

"Chill out," says Raven.

"I do not know how," Robin replies.

"We will show you," says Cyborg.

"Come with me."

"Try some tinkering," says Cyborg.

He hands Robin a tool.

"Yes, I see," Robin mutters.

"We can take this machine apart
and build something bigger and faster!"

"That is not what I meant," Cyborg says.

But Robin does not hear him.

He is already hard at work.

"Here is something simpler," says Starfire.

"It is a spa mask!"

She spreads green goo all over Robin's face.

"It is made out of pickles and cream cheese," says Starfire.

"Is this not relaxing?"

"No," says Robin.

"But with a few drops of acid, it could make a great weapon."

Beast Boy talks to Robin next.

"You have to stop thinking about work,"
Beast Boy says.

"Here. Sit down.

Be one with the couch."

"What do you mean?" Robin asks.

"Watch," says Beast Boy.

Beast Boy leans back.

He closes his eyes

and hums a little song.

Soon he is a part of the furniture!

Robin is confused,
but he is determined.
"I will master oneness
with the couch," he says.

Robin slouches.

He hums.

He starts to drift away.

"Can it be?" the Titans whisper.

"Is Robin really relaxing?"

Just then, a beep goes off.

Robin jumps up from the couch.

"Crime?!" he asks.

"No," says Cyborg.
"Just some popcorn."

29

The Teen Titans laugh.

"You may not be one with the couch,"

Beast Boy tells Robin,

"but you will always be one of us,

no matter what."

What a great team!

TEEN TITANS GO!

BOYS VERSUS GIRLS

Adapted by Jennifer Fox
Based on the episode "Boys vs. Girls"
written by John Loy

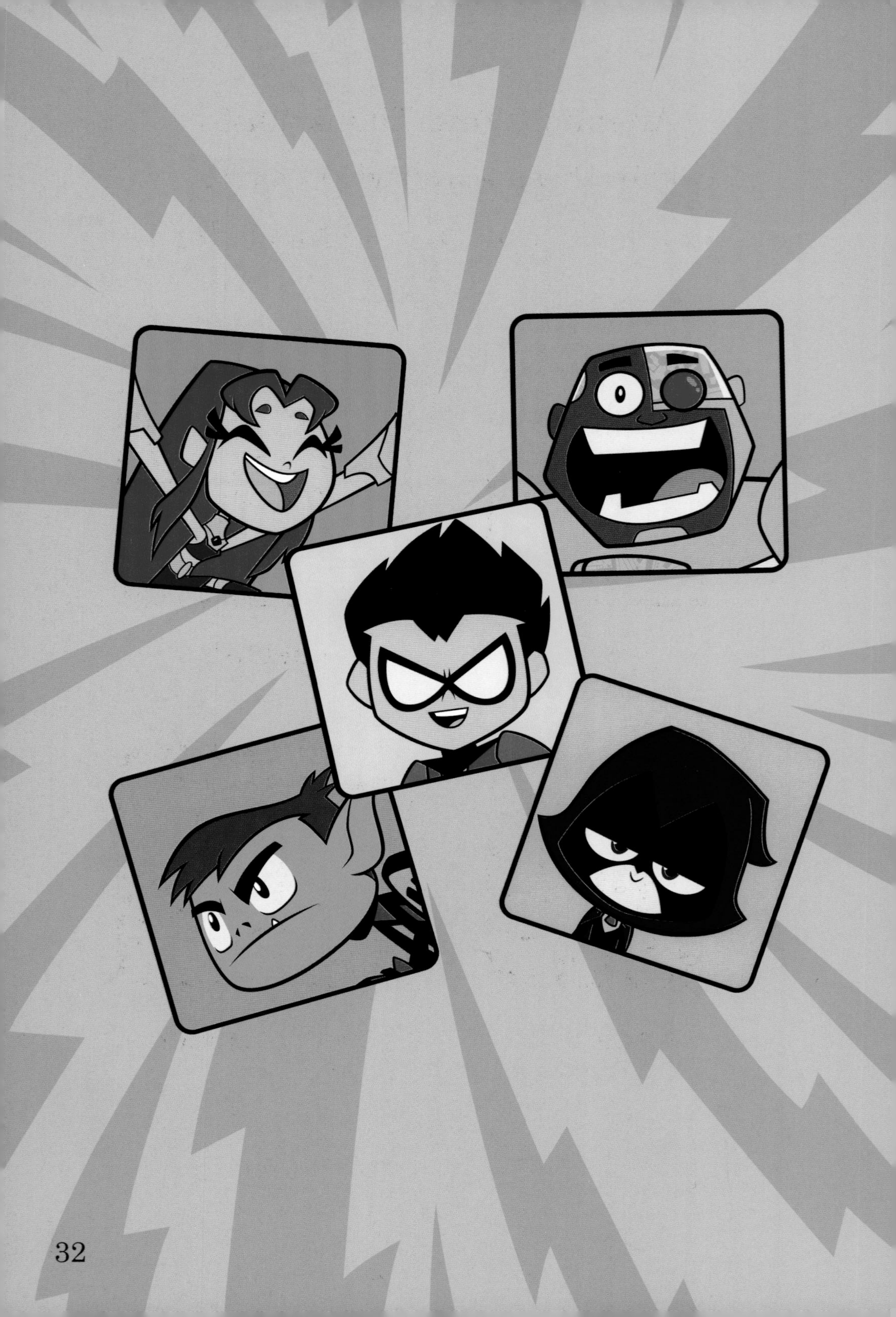

Attention, Teen Titans fans!
Look for these words when you read
this book. Can you spot them all?

car

cheetah

truck

cootie catcher

VRRRRM! VRRRRM! VRRRRM!
Beast Boy zooms around
on a crazy car.

BURP!
Cyborg lets out
a huge stinky burp.

"We are being such boys!"
Robin says.

"BOYS! BOYS! BOYS!"
they shout.

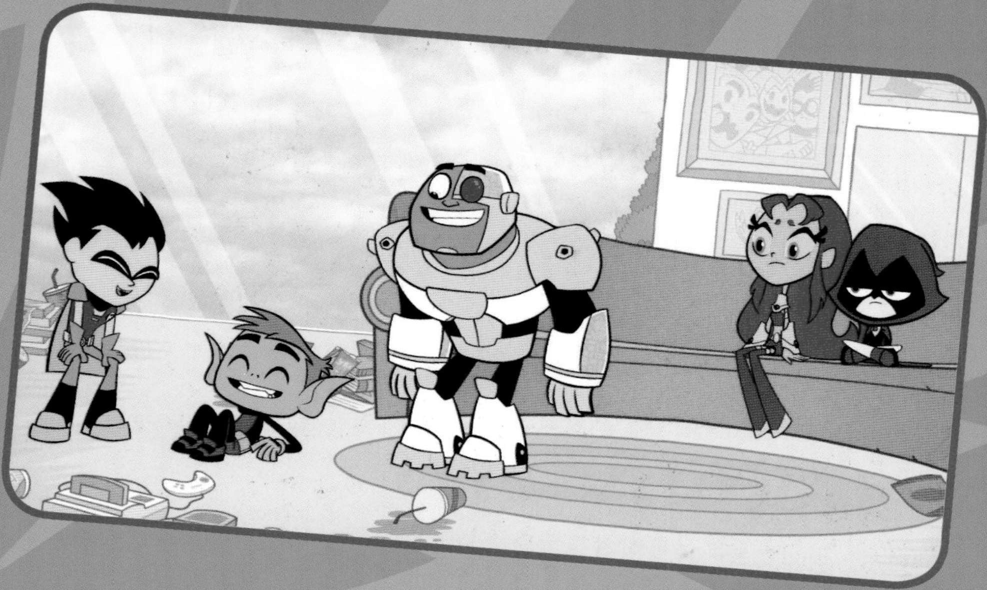

"Quiet!" Raven yells.

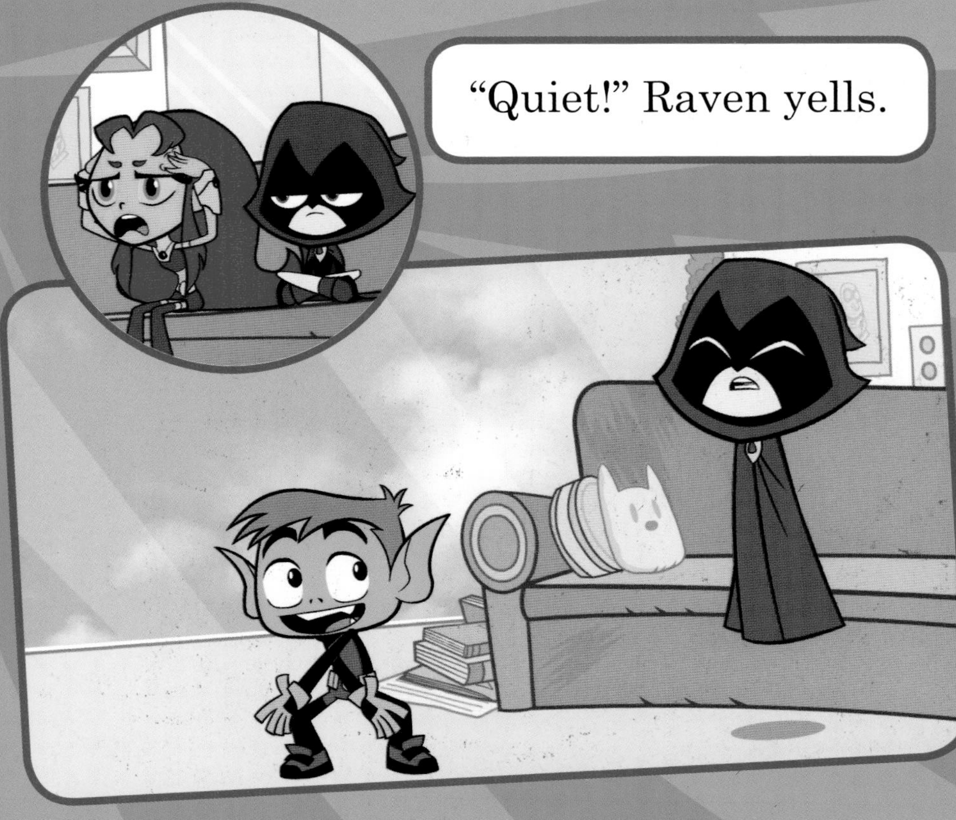

"What is her problem?"
Cyborg asks.

"Girls have cooties!"
Robin says.
"Boys are better than girls."

"Prove it," Raven says.

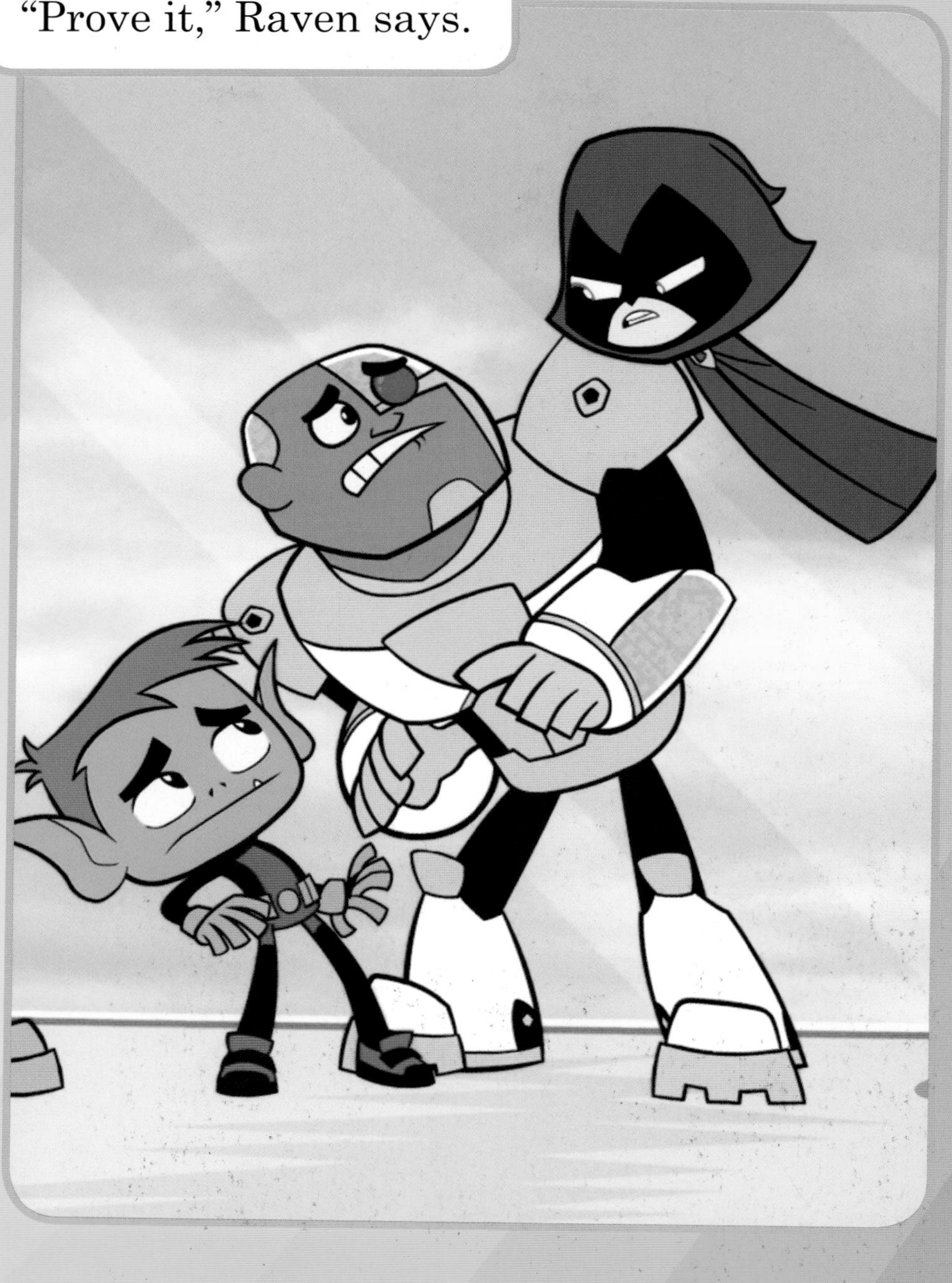

It is time for a contest.
It is boys versus girls.

First, Beast Boy
and Starfire race.

"It is cheetah time,"
Beast Boy says.
Starfire flies by
him so fast.

Next, Robin and Raven
must solve a math problem.
"You are going down,"
Robin says.

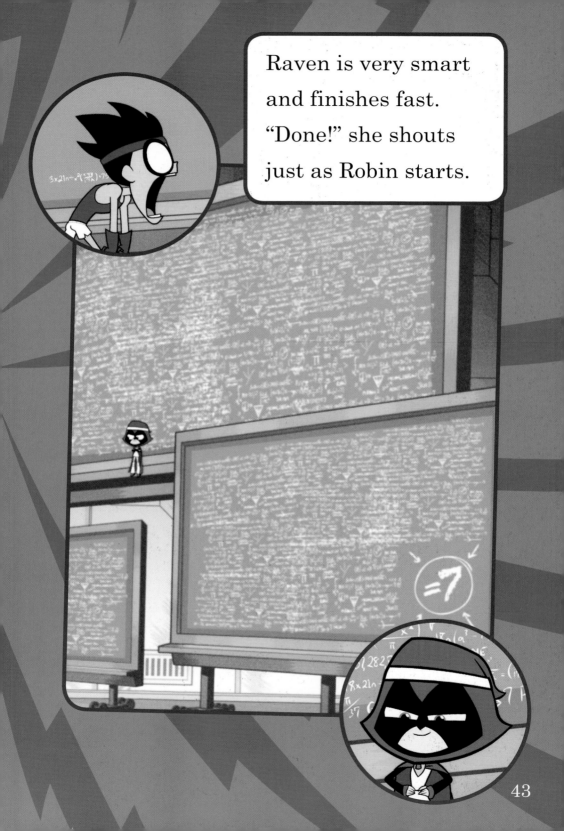

Raven is very smart and finishes fast. "Done!" she shouts just as Robin starts.

Last, the teams have a tug-of-war.

Cyborg transforms into a turbo truck to make him strong.

44

It is a close contest.

Raven's magic makes
the girls stronger
than the boys!

BOYS 0

GIRLS 3

The girls win!
Cyborg and Beast Boy
join the girls team.

"GIRLS! GIRLS! GIRLS!"
they shout.

Robin still wants to prove boys are better than girls. He has a plan.

He sneaks into a lab
and steals some cooties.

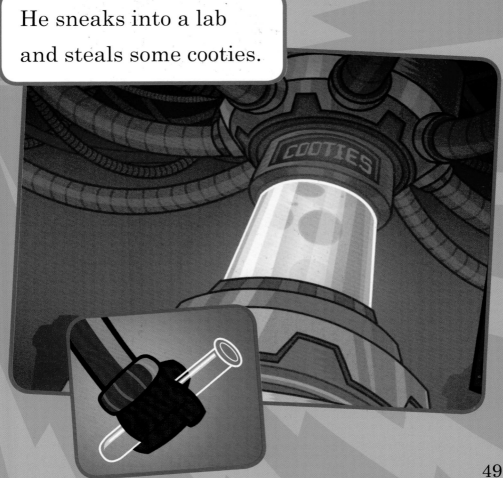

That night,
Robin slips cooties
into the girls' rooms.

He thinks this will make the boys better!

The next day,
Raven and Starfire
feel itchy.

"My skin is crawling,"
Raven says.

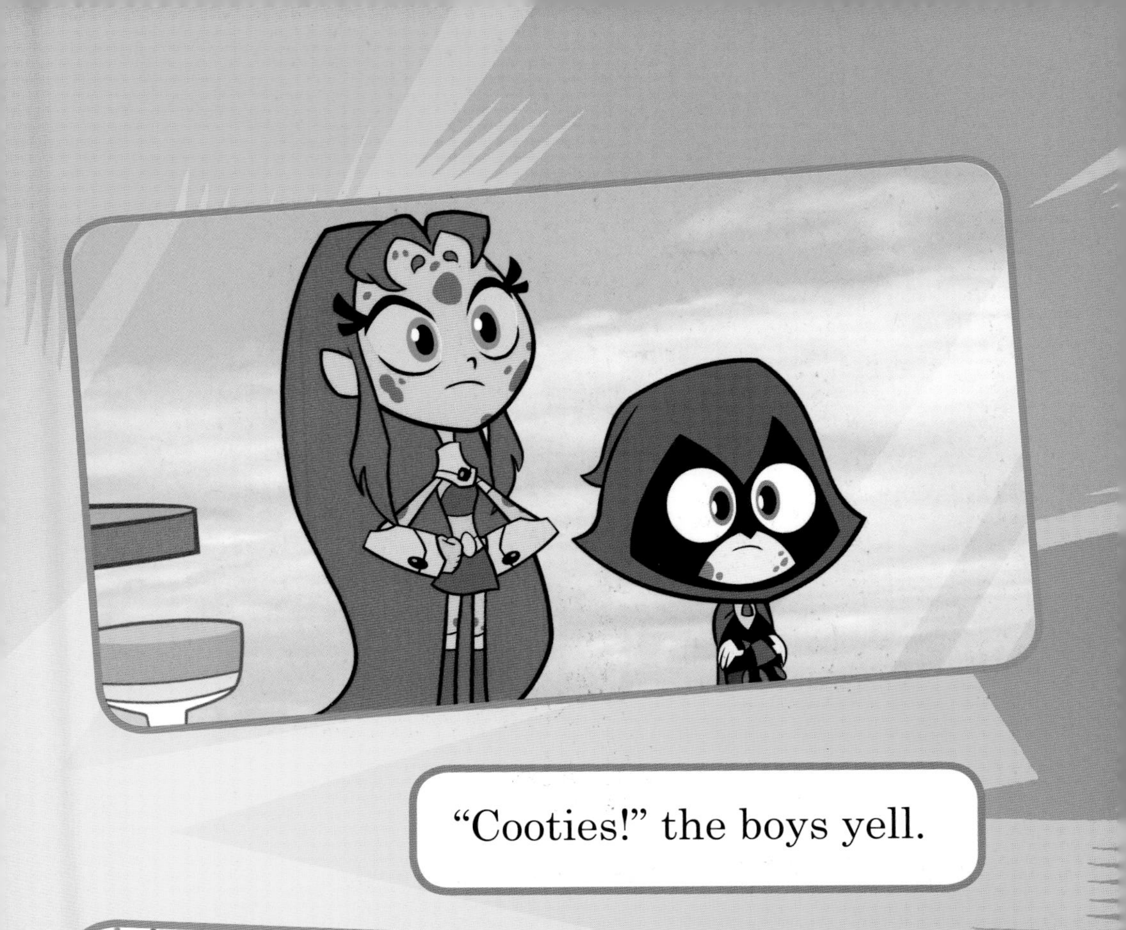

“Cooties!” the boys yell.

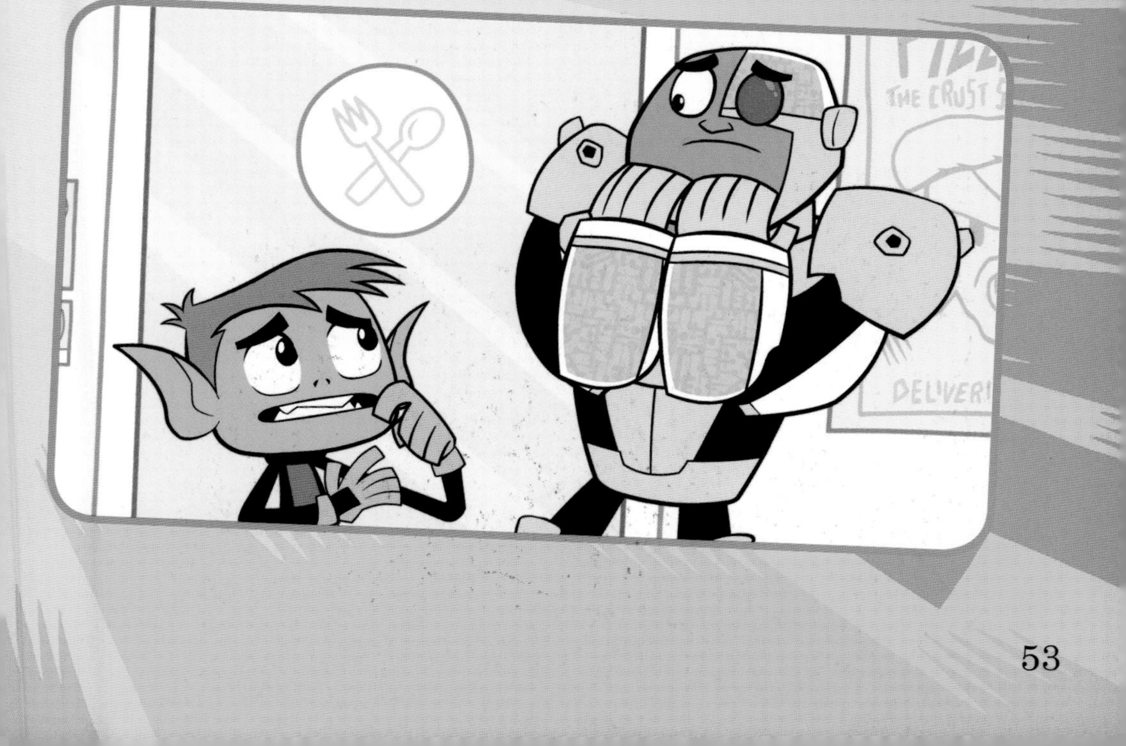

Robin has the cure.
"A cootie catcher!" he says.

"Give us the catcher," Starfire says.

"Only if you say
boys are the best," Robin says.
"Never!" Raven and Starfire say.

The girls have an idea.
They will catch the boys
and give them cooties, too.

"Run!" Robin shouts.

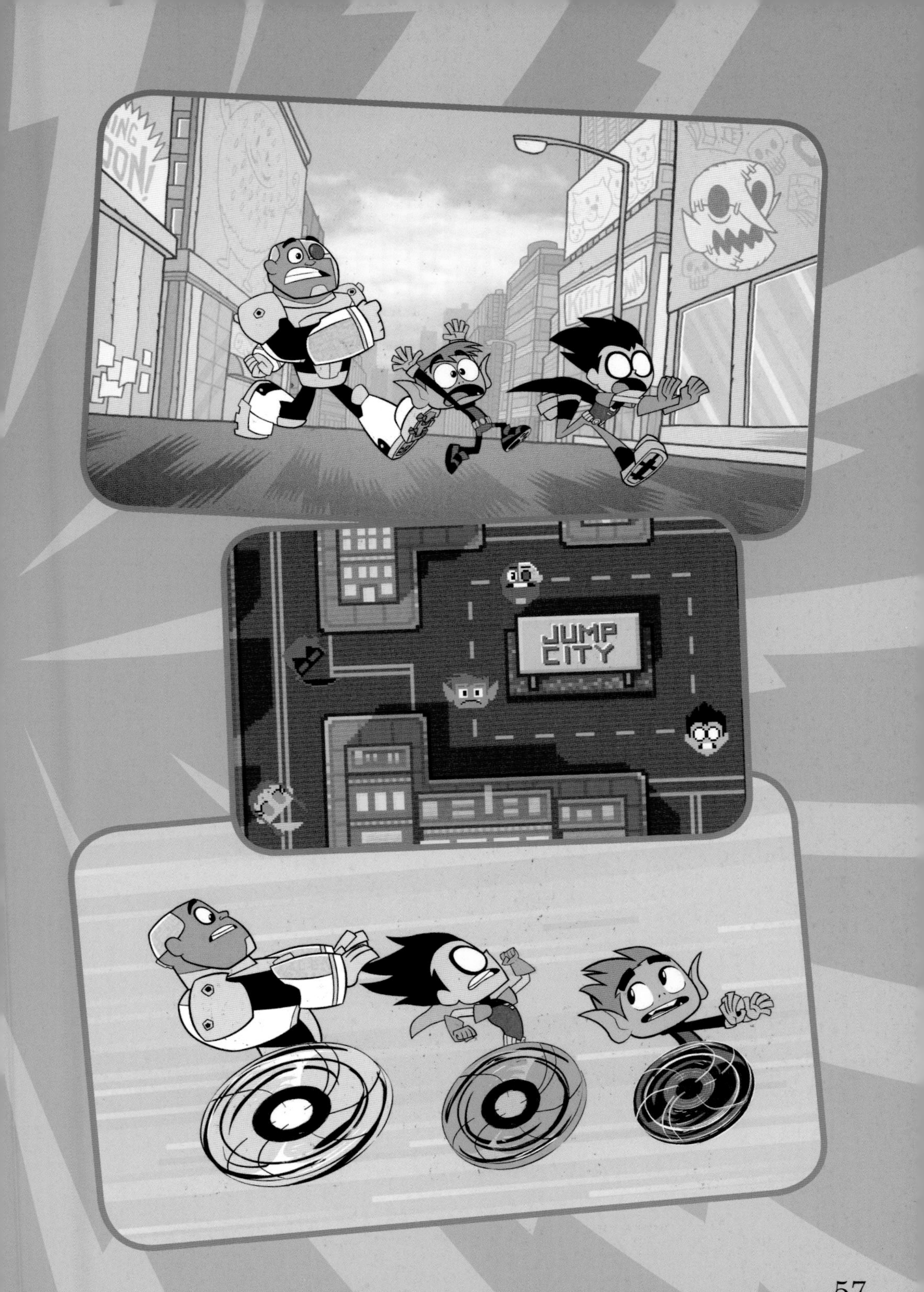
JUMP
CITY

The girls are fast.
They catch the boys.
"Now we all have
cooties," Starfire says.

Robin uses the cootie catcher!

The team is cured!

The boys and girls agree that the best thing is being cootie-free.

BRAIN FOOD

Adapted by Jennifer Fox
Based on the episode "Brain Food"
written by John Loy

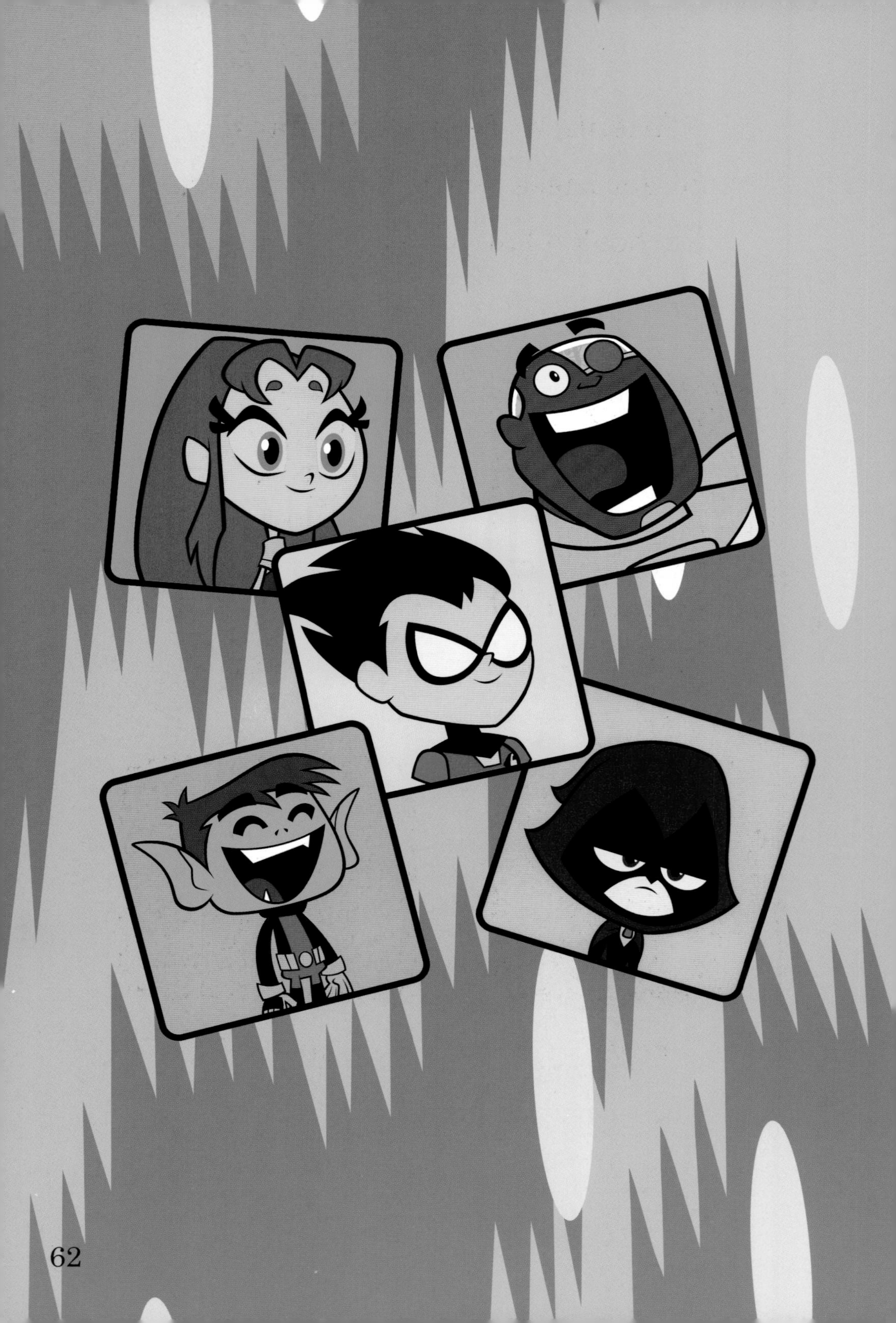

Attention, Teen Titans fans!
Look for these words when you read
this book. Can you spot them all?

asteroid

ocean

robot

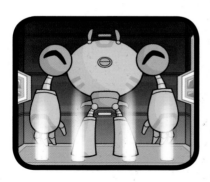

butterfly

"Okay, Titans!" says Robin. "An asteroid is about to smash into Earth."

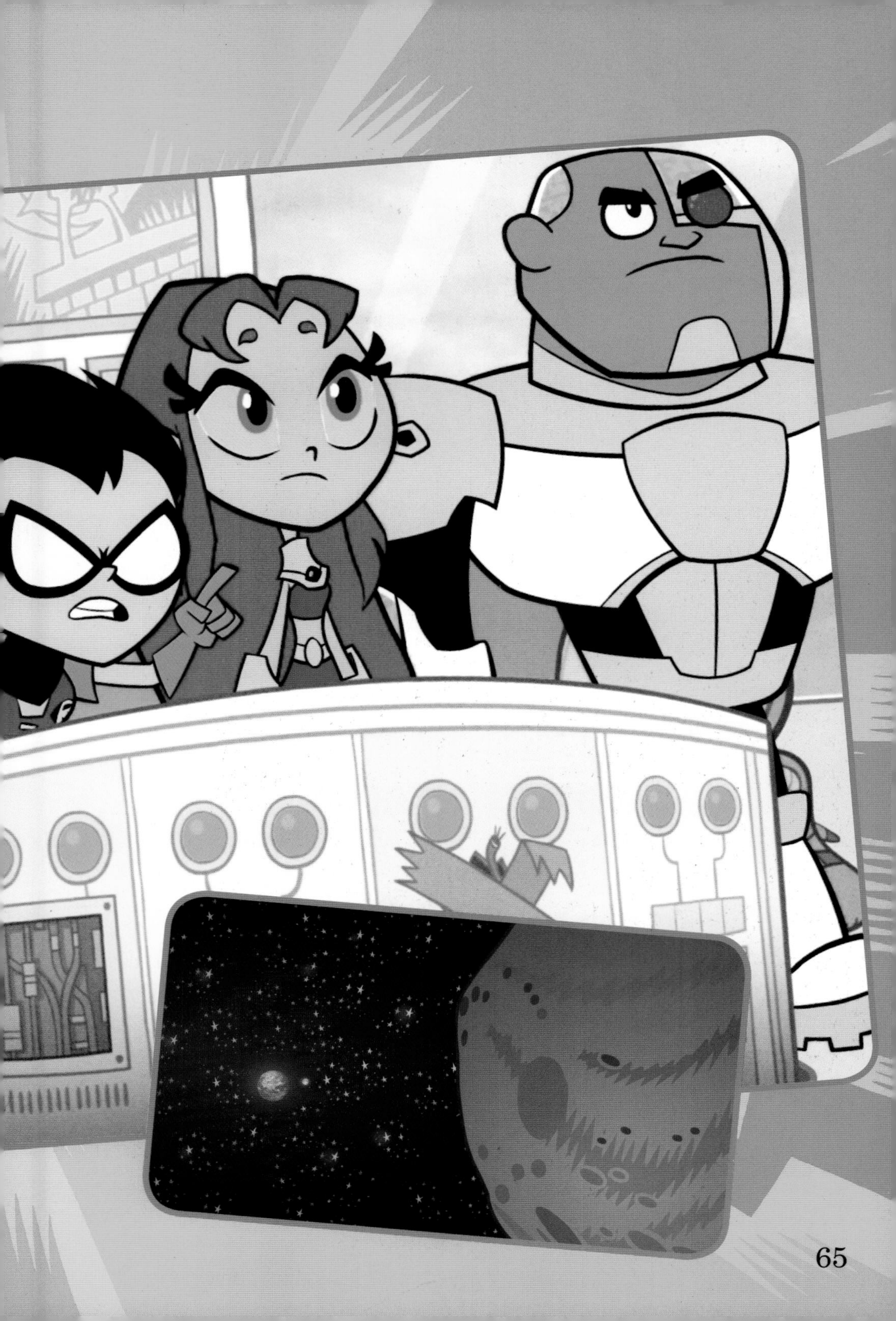

"Raven, see how big it is,"
says Robin.

"Starfire, find out what it is made of. Cyborg, build something to blow it up."

"Dude, what about me?" asks Beast Boy.

"Hold this," says Robin.

"Or give Silkie a bath."

"Why do I never get
the big jobs?"
asks Beast Boy.

"You do not know how to do a lot of stuff," says Cyborg.

It is true.

Beast Boy breaks things.

He pushes when he should pull.

He wants to be smart
like the other Titans.
But he thinks brain food
goes in your ear.

73

Beast Boy grabs
Raven's spell book.
"I am going to make
myself smarter!" he says.

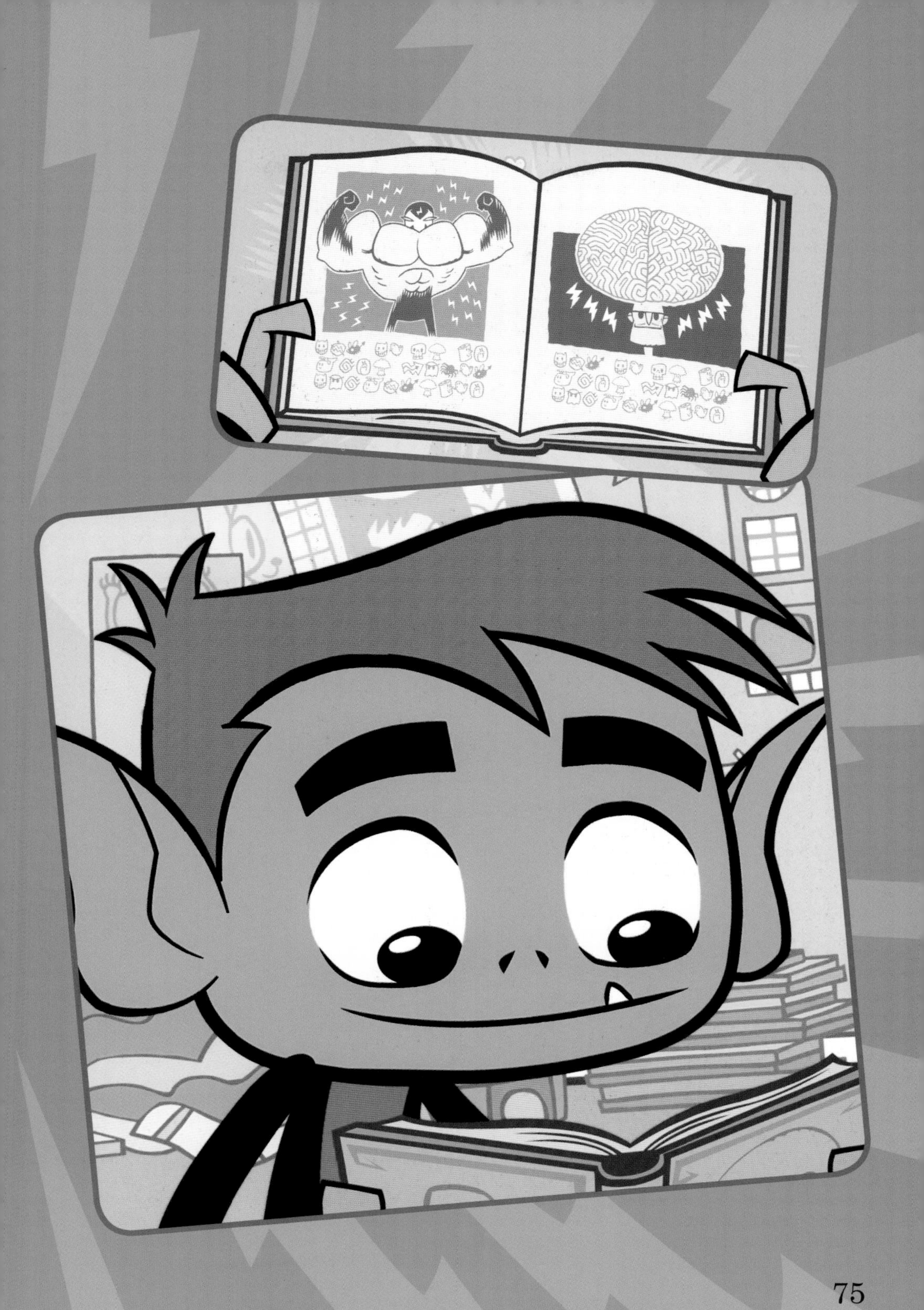

Beast Boy says the magic words.
But something goes wrong.

Beast Boy is not smarter.

So he tries a spell to make the
other Titans lose their smarts.
It works!

"These bowls do not work!" says Cyborg.

"Hey! Where is my foot?" asks Robin.

The asteroid is still speeding toward Earth.

"Look!" shouts Robin.

"Beast Boy!

We need you,"

say the other Titans.

Beast Boy thinks fast.

"Gravity is pulling the rock," he says.

"And the ocean controls gravity.
So we have to fight the ocean!"

"Titans, go!" Robin shouts.
The Titans attack the ocean.
They clobber currents
and smack shells.

"It is not working, Beast Boy!"
Robin says.

Someone has a better plan. Silkie builds a robot to blast the space rock to bits.

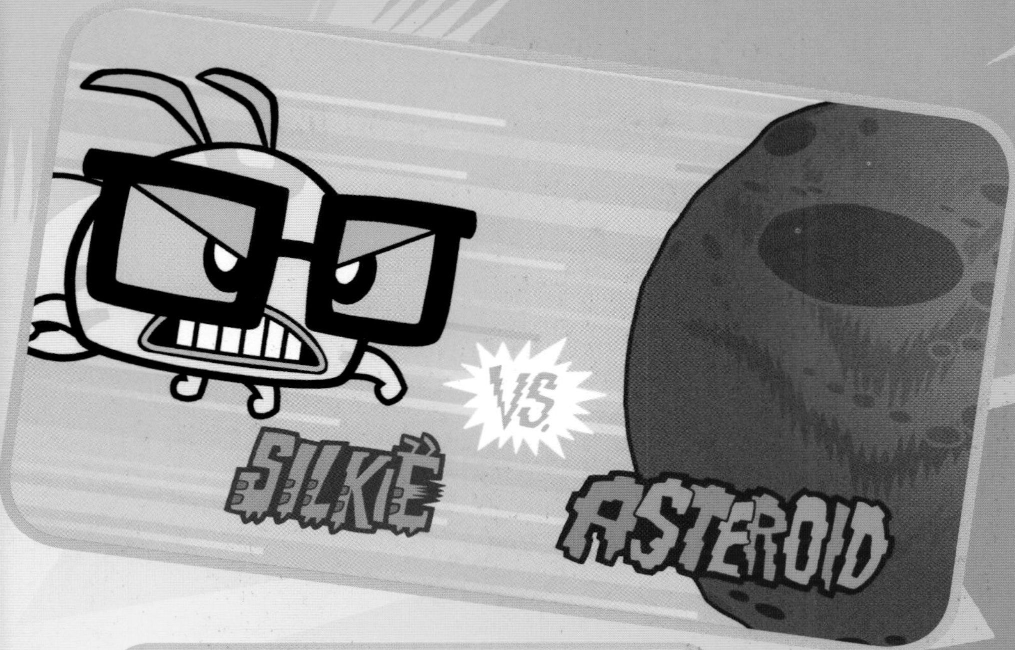
VS.
SILKIE
ASTEROID

The worm saves the day!

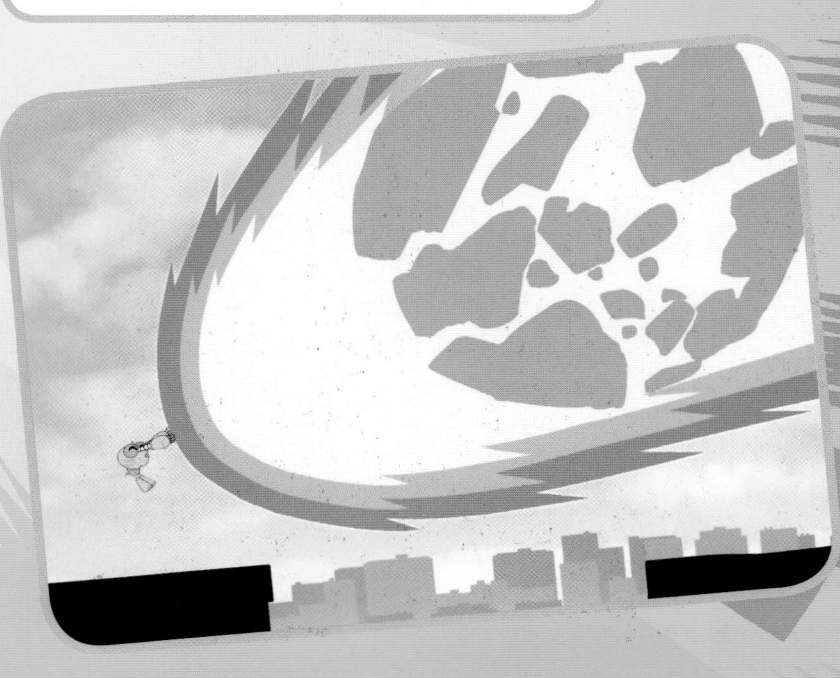

"Look!
The rock went home,"
Cyborg says.

Planet Earth and
the not-so-smart
Titans are safe...

...until they see a butterfly.
They run into a window.
SPLAT!

TOOTH FAIRY FREAK-OUT

Adapted by Jennifer Fox
Based on the episode "The Dignity of Teeth"
written by Ben Gruber

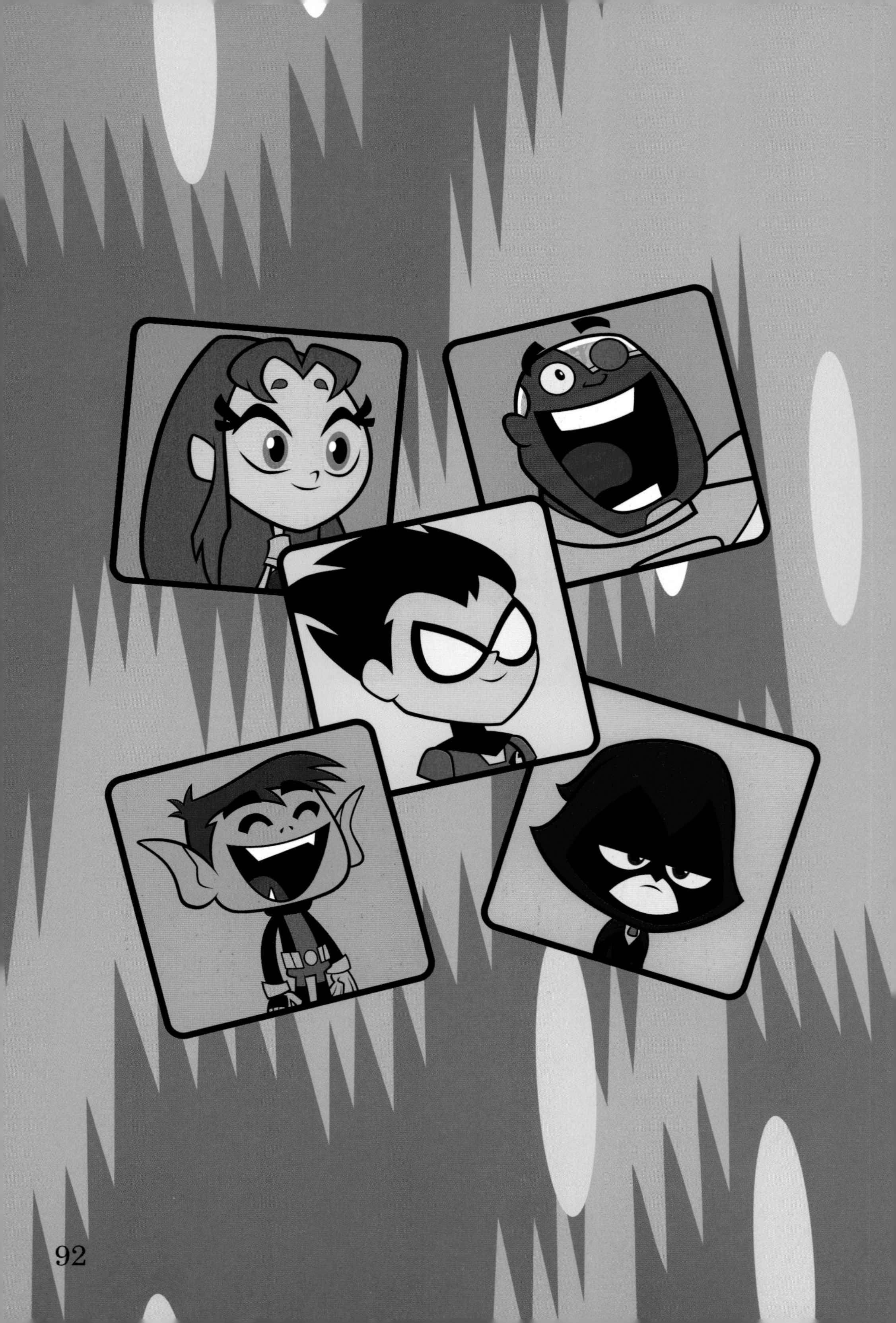

Attention, Teen Titans fans!
Look for these words when you read
this book. Can you spot them all?

dolls

breath

cavity

money

"What is that smell?" yells Robin.
"Beast Boy's onion and garlic
stew," says Cyborg.

Robin gasps.
"Your breath is TOXIC, Titans!"

"You guys need to brush,"
Robin says.

The Titans get to work.
"Not your hair!" Robin cries.
"Your TEETH!"

Beast Boy opens his mouth wide.
"Look, a cavity!" Robin shouts.
"That tooth needs to go."

"No way," says Beast Boy.
"I love ALL my teeth!"

Cyborg tells Beast Boy that the Tooth Fairy brings money for teeth.

"A fairy...how sweet!"
says Starfire.
"I think it is creepy,"
says Raven.

That night, Beast Boy leaves his tooth under his pillow.

The next day he looks. "I got paid!" he cries.

He starts losing teeth on purpose to get more money.

The other Teen Titans see
Beast Boy's cool new sunglasses
and piles of money.

They start losing teeth
on purpose, too.

Raven still thinks that the Tooth Fairy is creepy.

Soon the Teen Titans look like toothless zombies. "More money!" they yell.

"That is it," Raven shouts.

"We are getting your teeth back."

The Tooth Fairy's lair
is full of teeth.

"Creepy!" Raven says.
The Tooth Fairy
flies into the room!

"What do you do with
all the teeth?" Raven asks.
"Make jewelry?" Robin guesses.

"Dress them up like dolls?"
asks Starfire.

"No, I EAT them!"
the Tooth Fairy says.

"Ew," Raven says.
"Give my friends
their teeth back!"

The Tooth Fairy makes
a deal with Raven.

"We will have a contest.
If you win, you get
your friends' teeth back.
If you lose, I get your teeth, too!"

113

"Fine," says Raven.
"What is the contest?"

"An eating contest!"
cries the Tooth Fairy.
"We will eat TEETH!"

Raven tastes a tooth.

"Wow," she says. "That is good!"

Raven shovels teeth in her mouth.

In a flash,
her pile is gone.
Raven wins!

The Tooth Fairy gives back
the Teen Titans' teeth.

At home, the Teen Titans thank Raven for saving their teeth.

"You were right," Cyborg says. "You cannot put a price on your teeth."

"No," says Raven…

"...but you can eat them!"

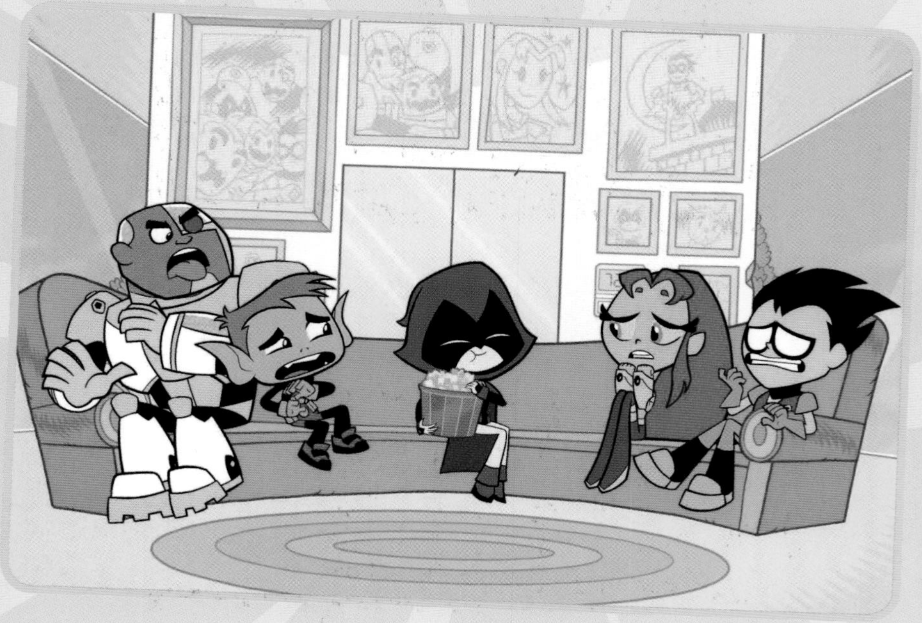

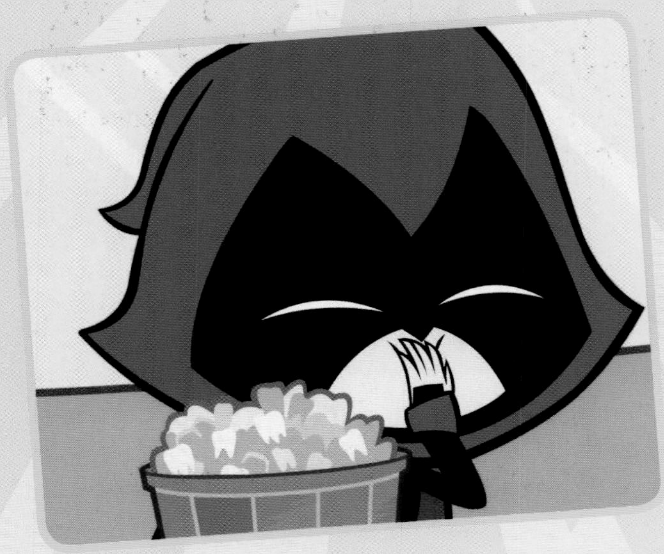

Written by Magnolia Belle

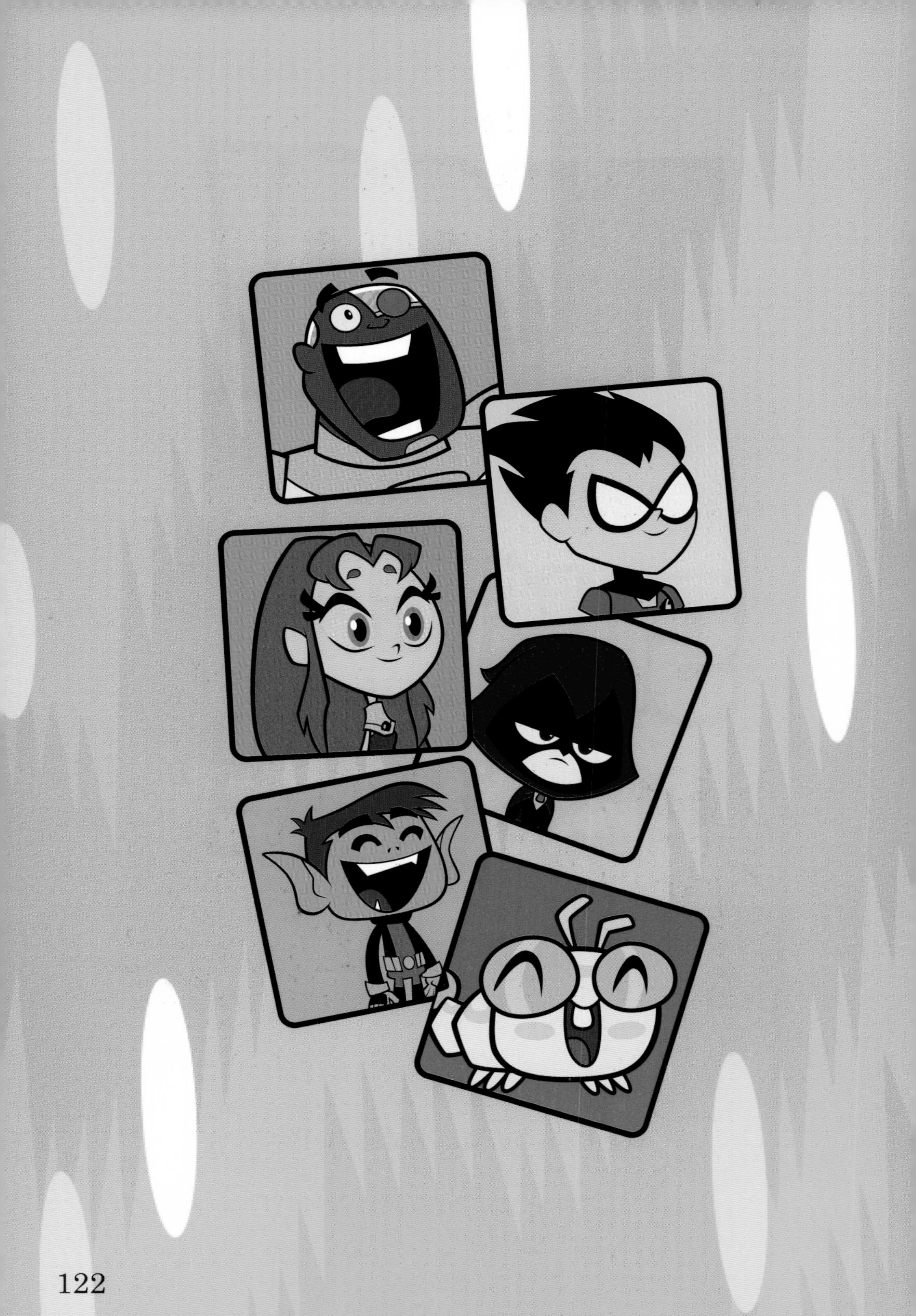

Attention, Teen Titans fans!
Look for these words when you read
this book. Can you spot them all?

berries

swimming

robot

sword

Silkie is the quiet, little pet of the Teen Titans.

Starfire takes care of Silkie and loves him more than anything.

Silkie loves Starfire a lot, too!

Silkie likes it when Starfire gives him baths and cleans behind his ears.

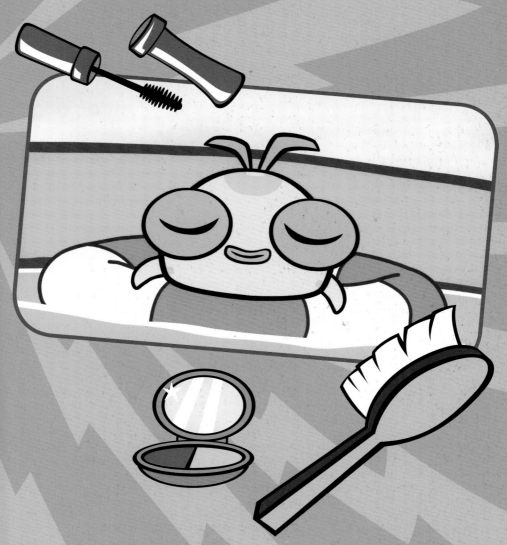

He also loves it when Starfire
tickles his tummy.
It makes him happy.

Starfire calls Silkie
her little baby.

Silkie's favorite food comes in a can.

If he gets really hungry,
he will eat almost anything.
But Silkie does not like tofu!

If Silkie eats berries
from Starfire's home planet,
he grows as big as a house!

Silkie wishes he could grow wings and fly.

He is also very good at avoiding danger!

Raven likes to play dress-up with Silkie.
She calls him Princess Silkie Soft.

Silkie also likes to play dress-up with Starfire.

Silkie loves it when
Cyborg reads to him...

...and when Beast Boy takes him swimming.

Beast Boy also likes to make himself look like Silkie!

One time, magic turned Silkie into a genius.

While Silkie was a genius,
he built a giant robot.

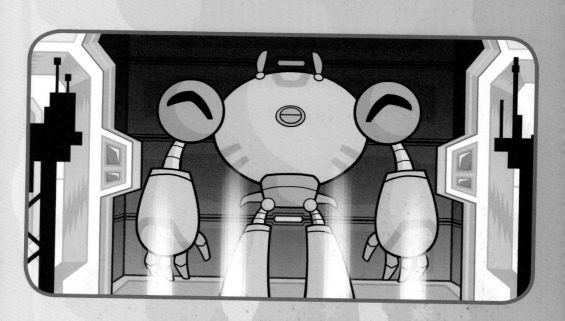

Silkie and his robot saved the world from a huge asteroid!

When Starfire goes on vacation, she asks the other Titans to babysit Silkie.

143

The Titans lose Silkie and have to look all over for him.

When Silkie gets lost,
he goes on many adventures.
Sophia is Silkie's new friend!

Sophia has a mean friend
named Carlos.
He locks up Sophia and Silkie!

Silkie is able to escape!

Carlos is so angry!
He challenges Silkie
to a sword fight.
Silkie wins!

When Silkie's adventures end,
he always returns home.

Starfire and the other Titans are so happy to see him!

PIZZA POWER

Adapted by Jennifer Fox
Based on the episode "Hey Pizza"
written by Amy Wolfram

Based on the episode "Truth, Justice, and What?"
written by Michael Jelenic and Aaron Horvath

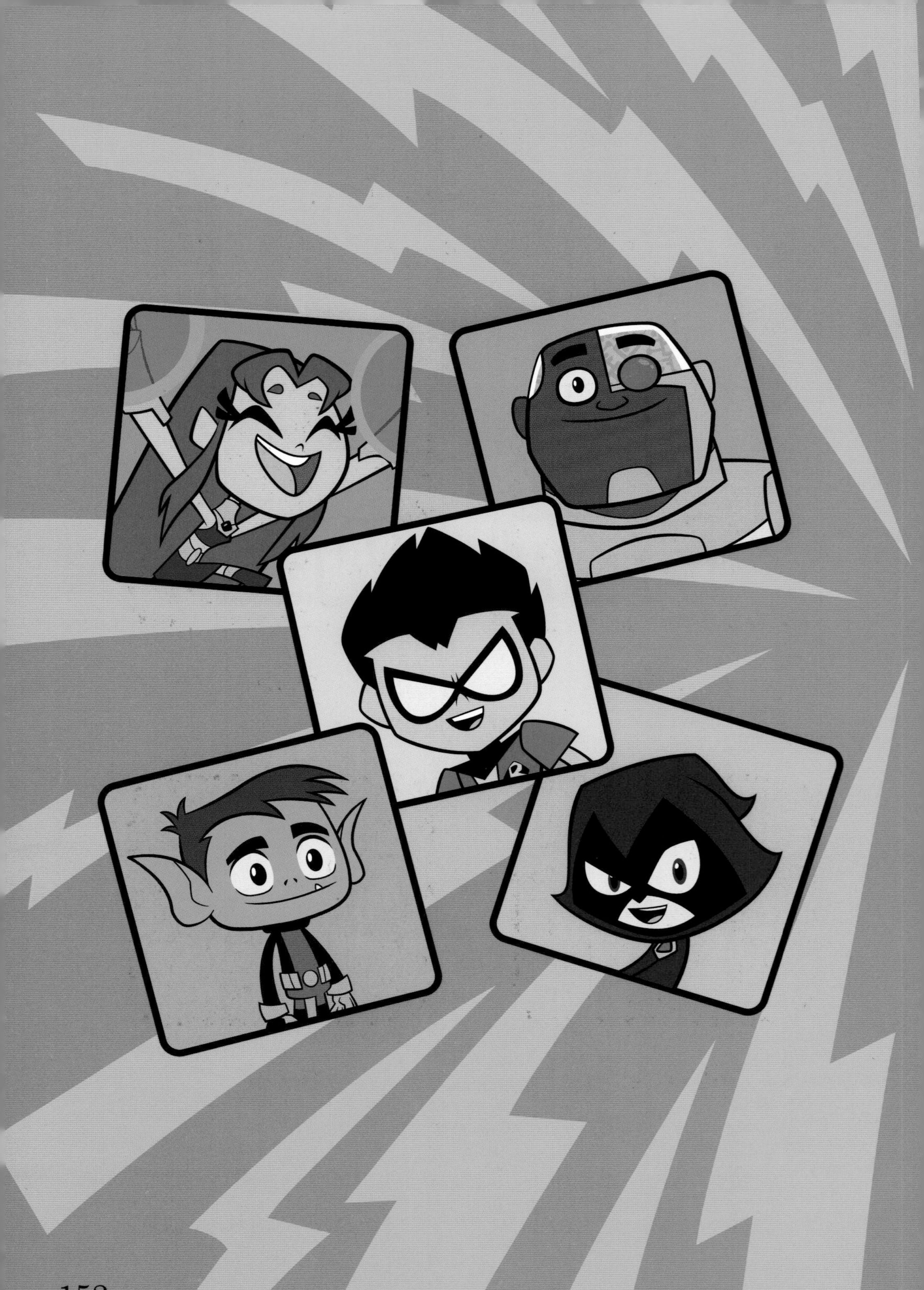

Attention, Teen Titans fans!
Look for these words when you read
this book. Can you spot them all?

burger

tank

pizza guy

pony

The Teen Titans
are super heroes
with superpowers.

Beast Boy goes wild.
Starfire blasts.

Cyborg smashes.

Raven casts spells.

And Robin?
No one knows
what he does.

What gives the Teen Titans
their powers?
Is it magic?

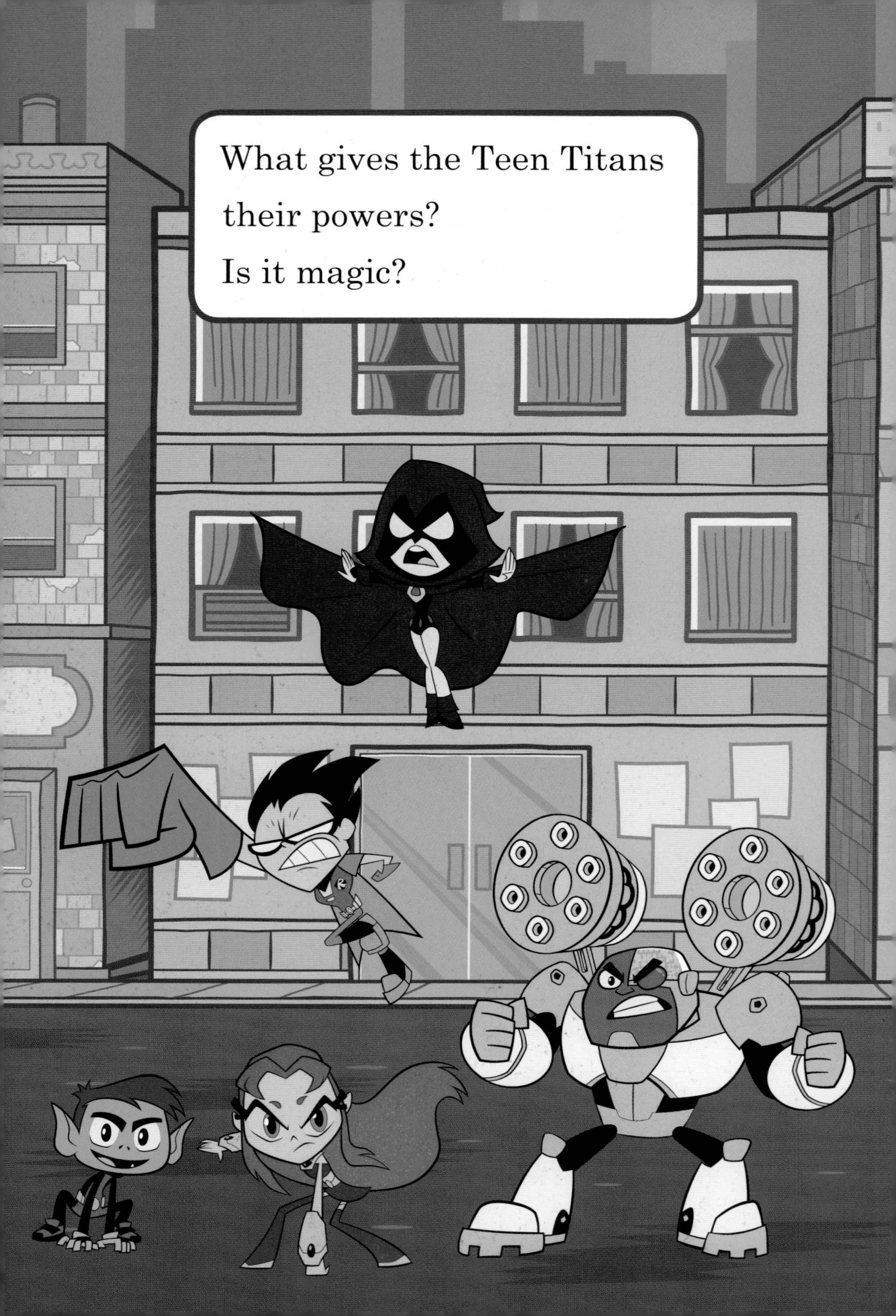

No!

It is...

PIZZA!

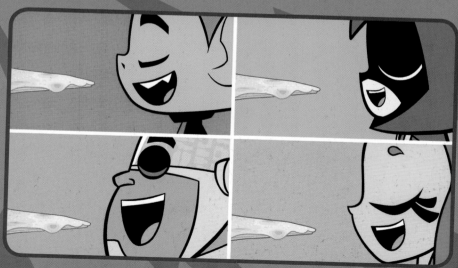

They eat it for
breakfast, lunch,
and dinner!
They eat it all day,
anytime!

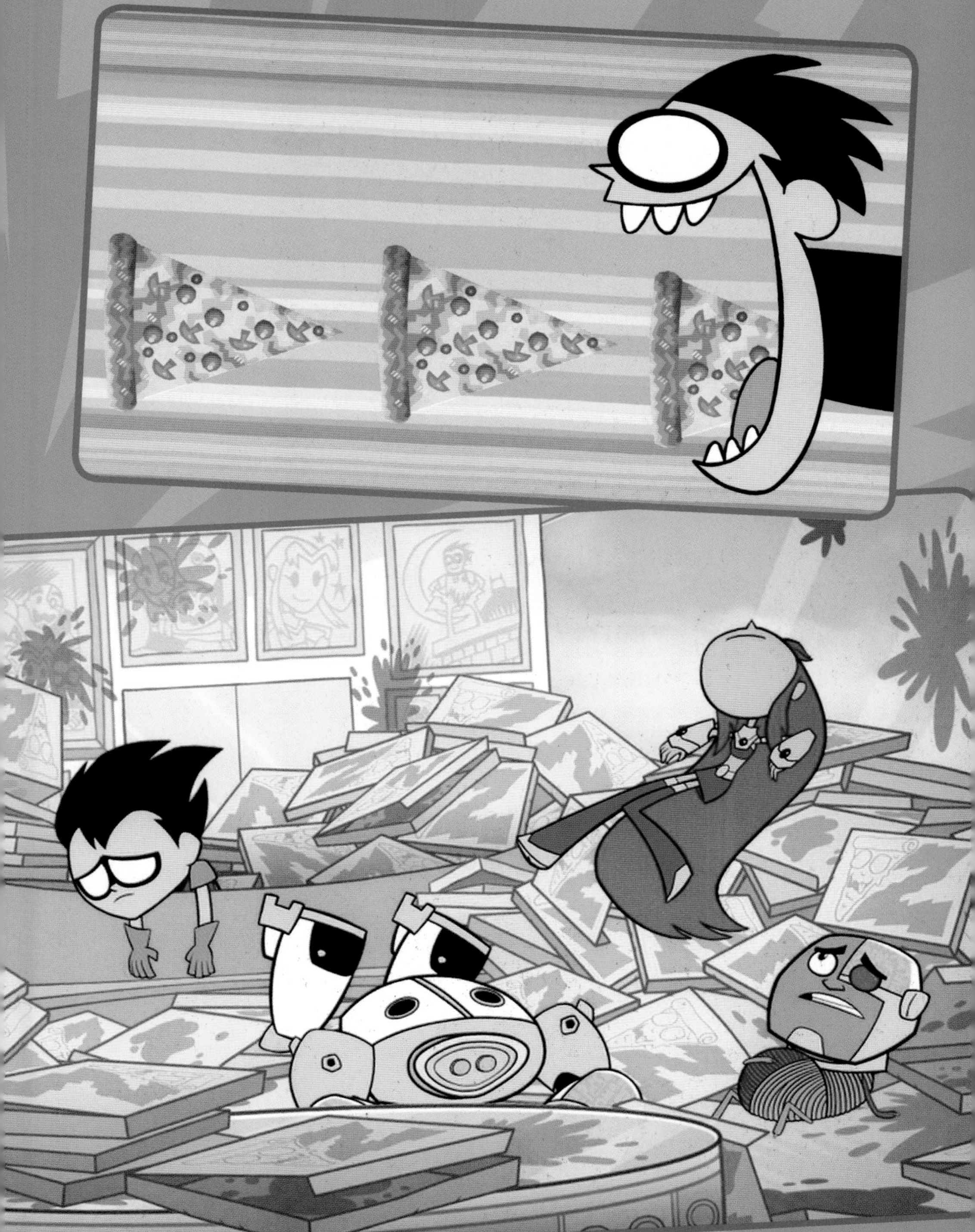

Burgers are beefy.
Burritos are zesty.

But hot, gooey pizza is the best...

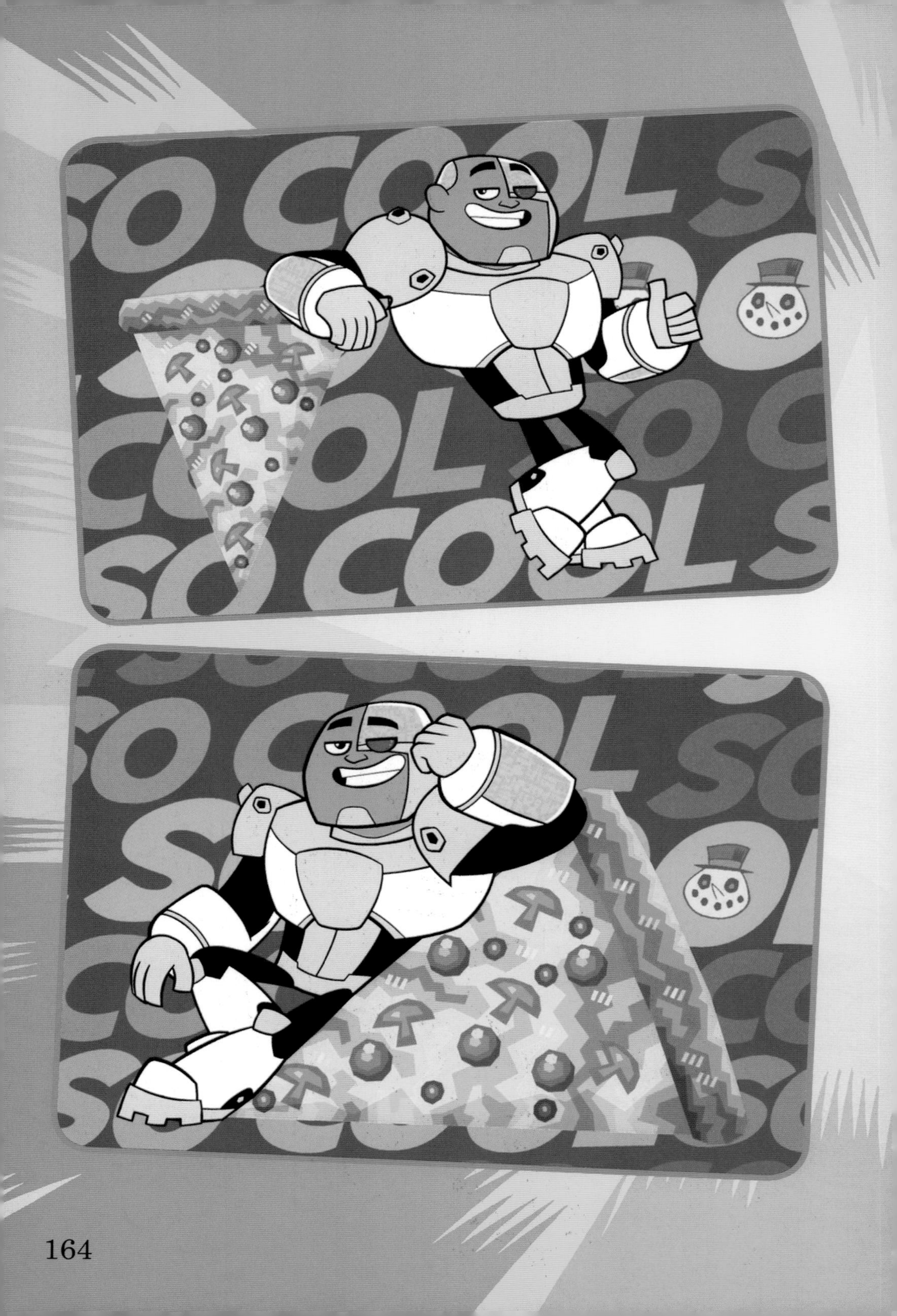
SO COOL

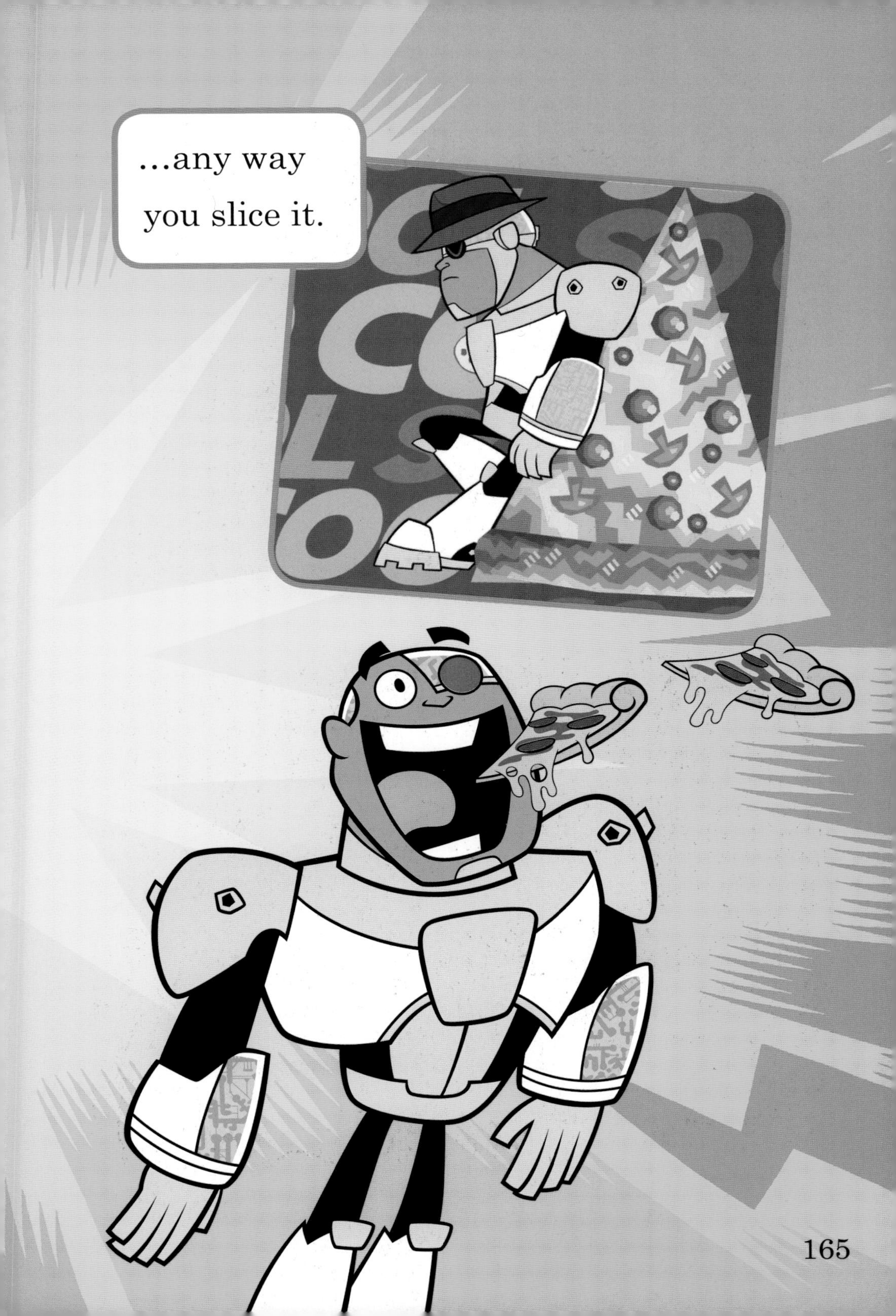
...any way you slice it.

It makes you
dance, jump,
burp, and go crazy!

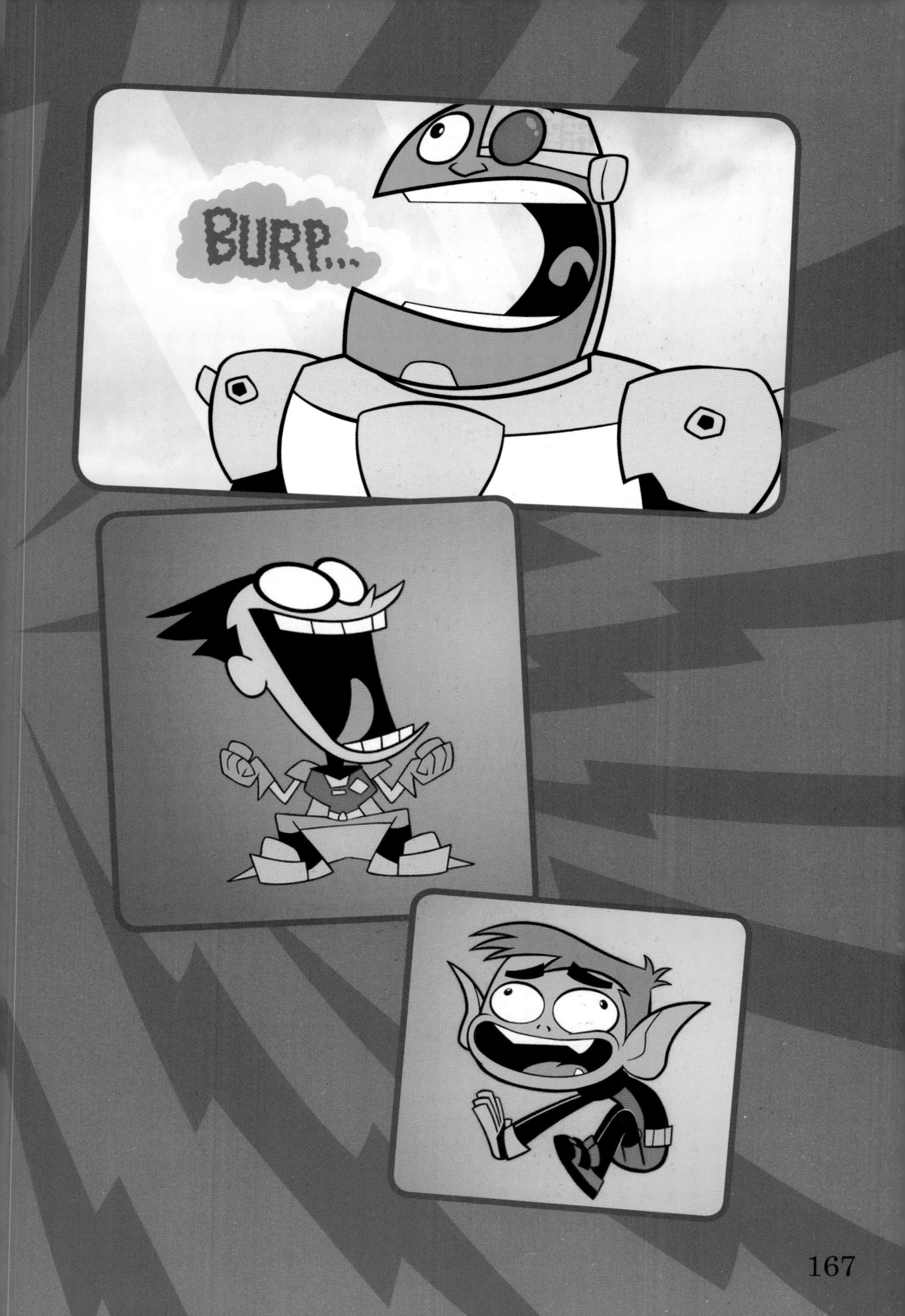
BURP...

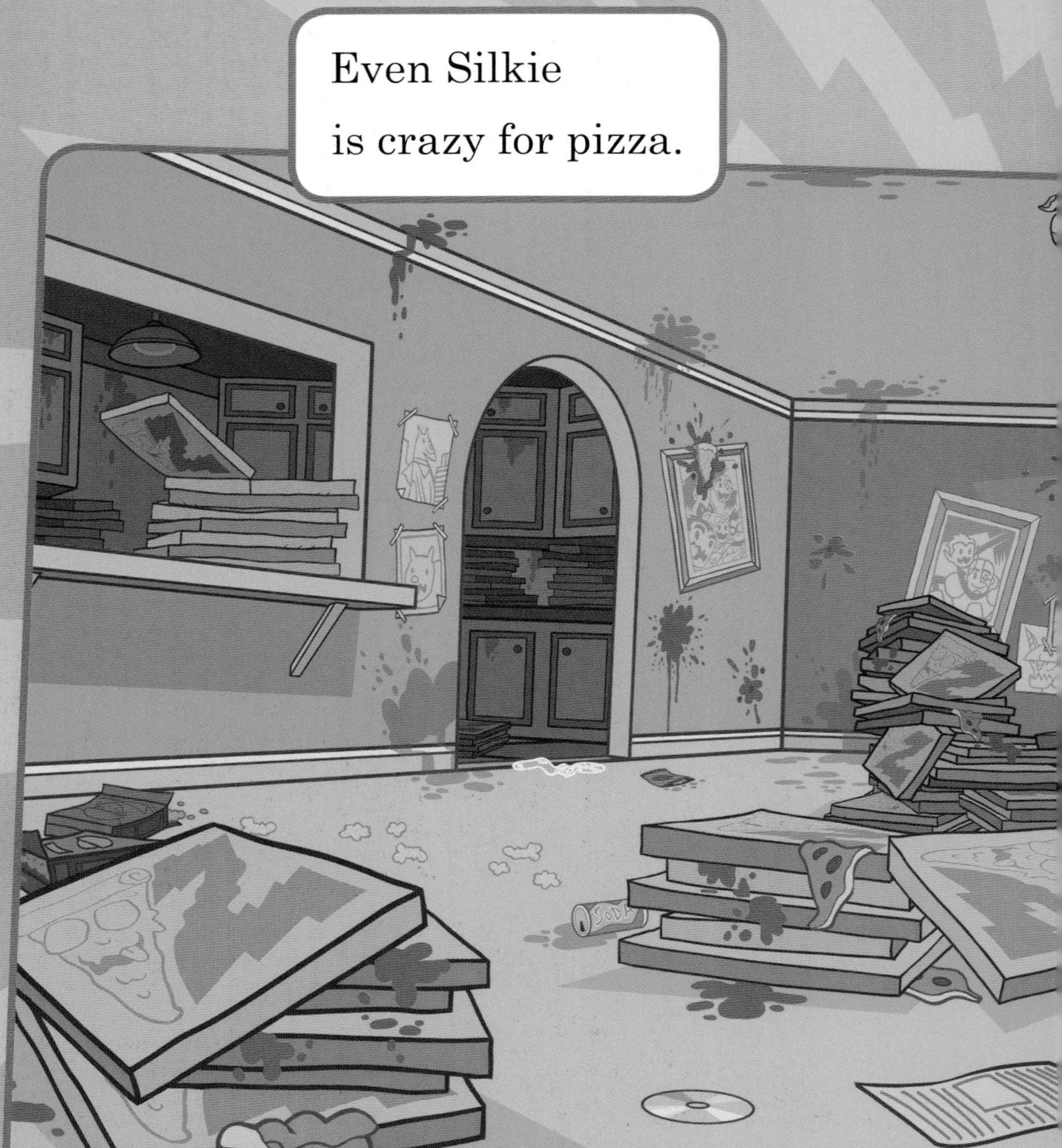
Even Silkie
is crazy for pizza.
SODA

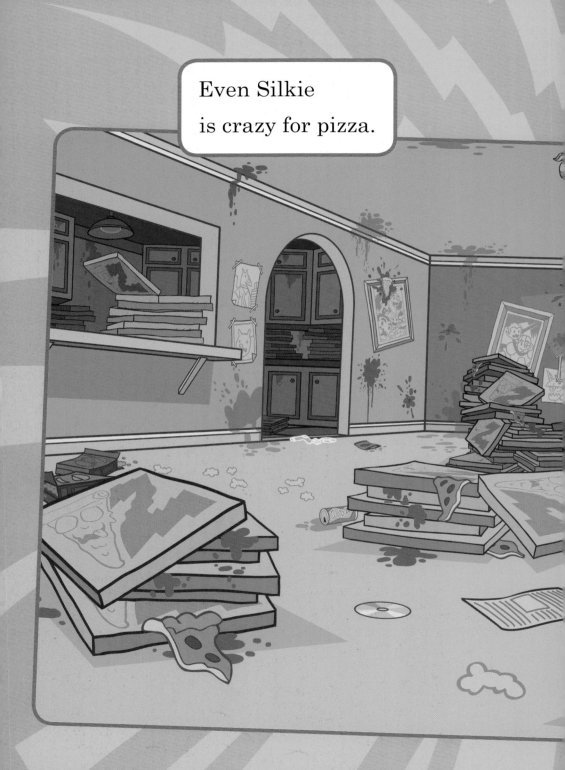

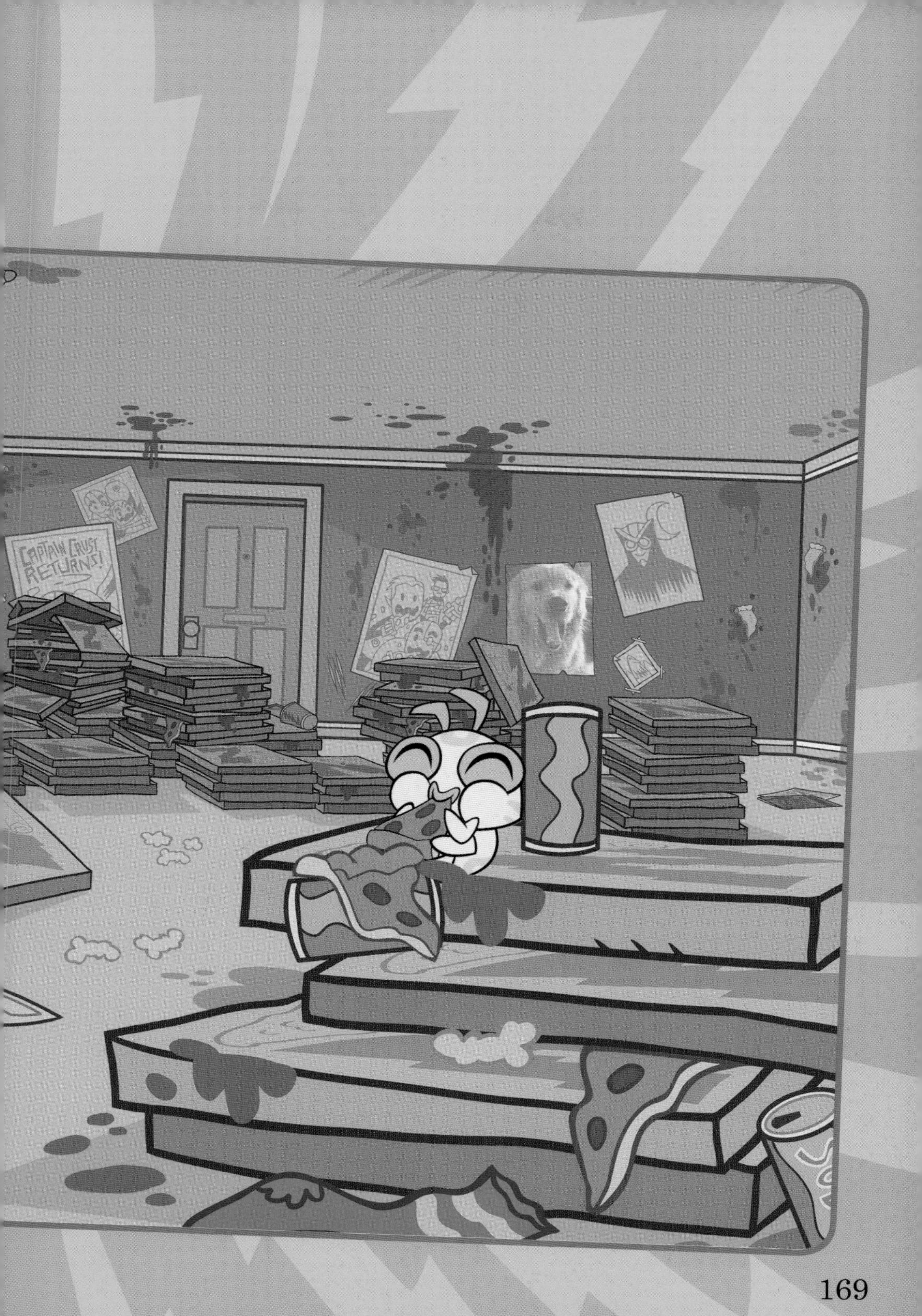
CAPTAIN CRUST RETURNS!

Cyborg's tank is empty.
"Let us get a pizza,"
says Beast Boy.

"If it is late, the pizza is free."

Too bad the pizza guy
is always on time.

"Hey, pizza!" says the pizza guy.

"Can I pay with a pony ride?"

asks Beast Boy.

However, there is one kind of pizza that scares the Teen Titans.

Is it the kind with
the weird little fish?
No...

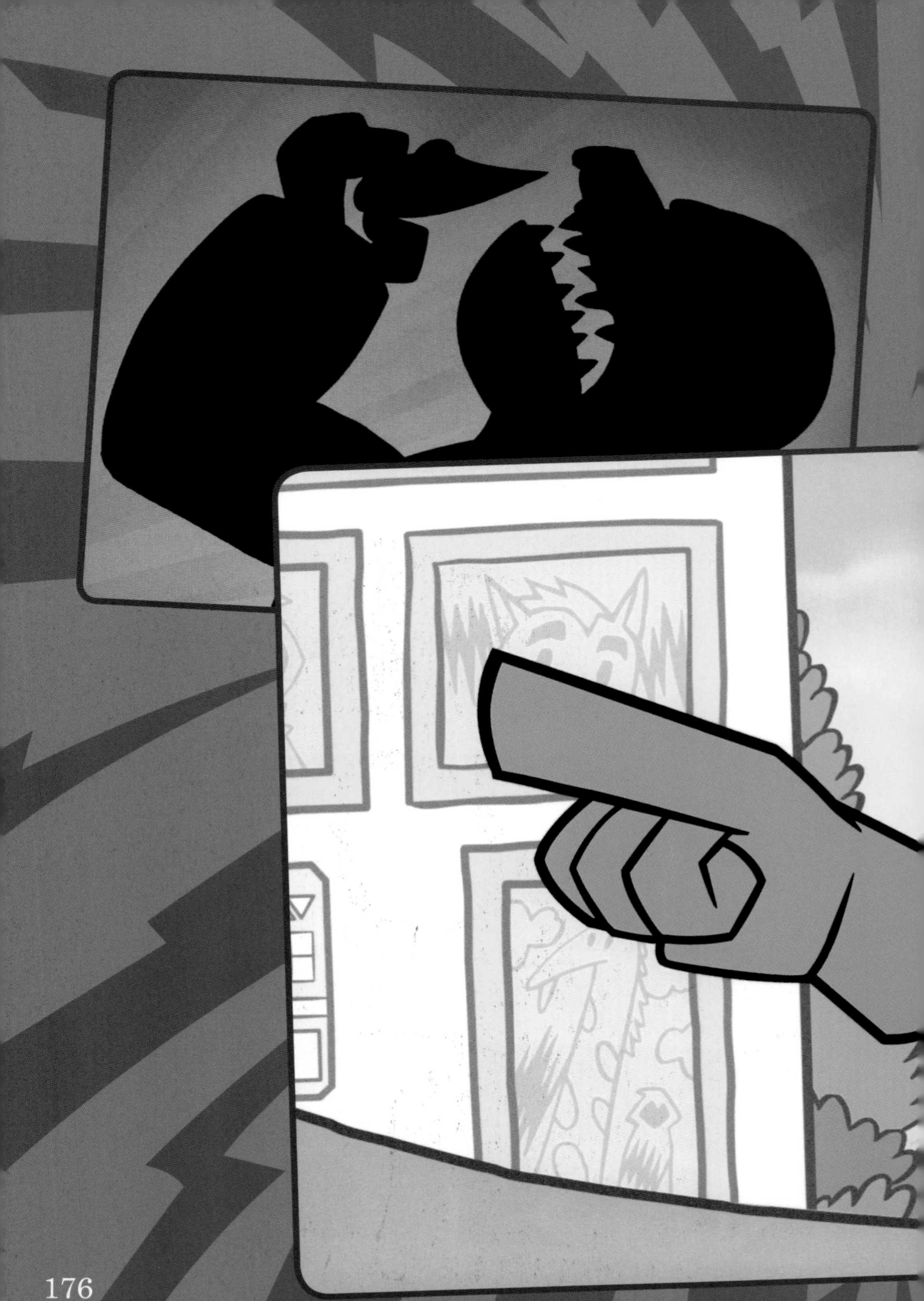

PIZZA MONSTER!!!!

Quick!

Close that box.

177

Phew.
That was close.

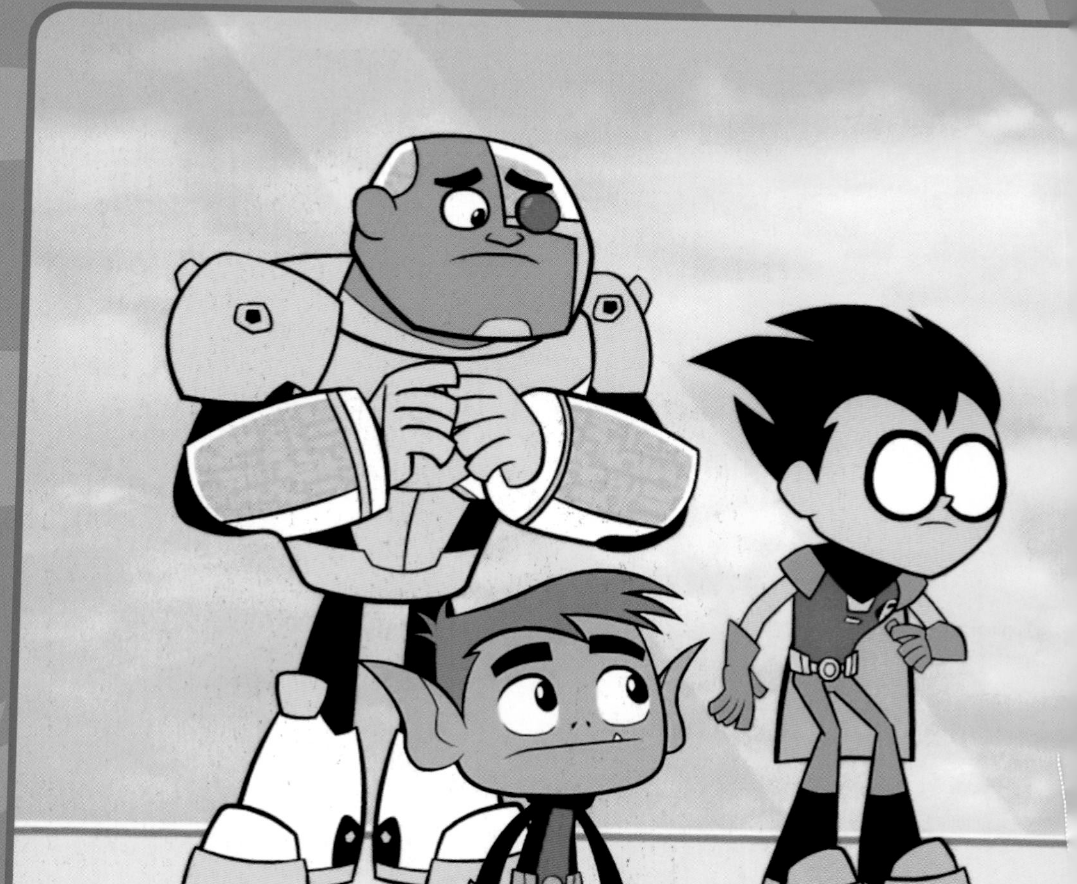

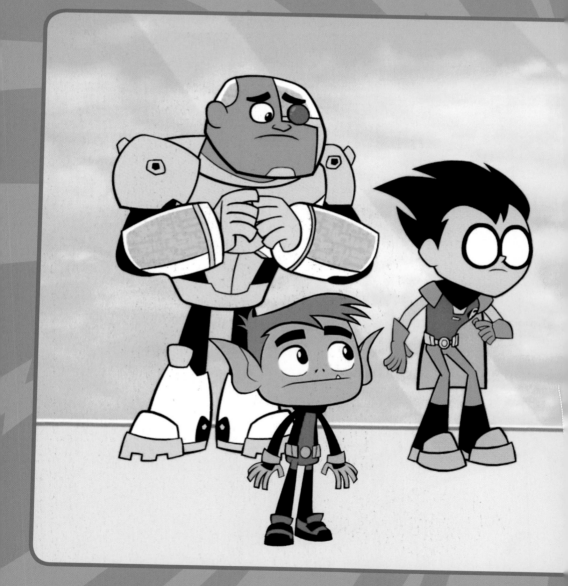

What will the Titans
do now?

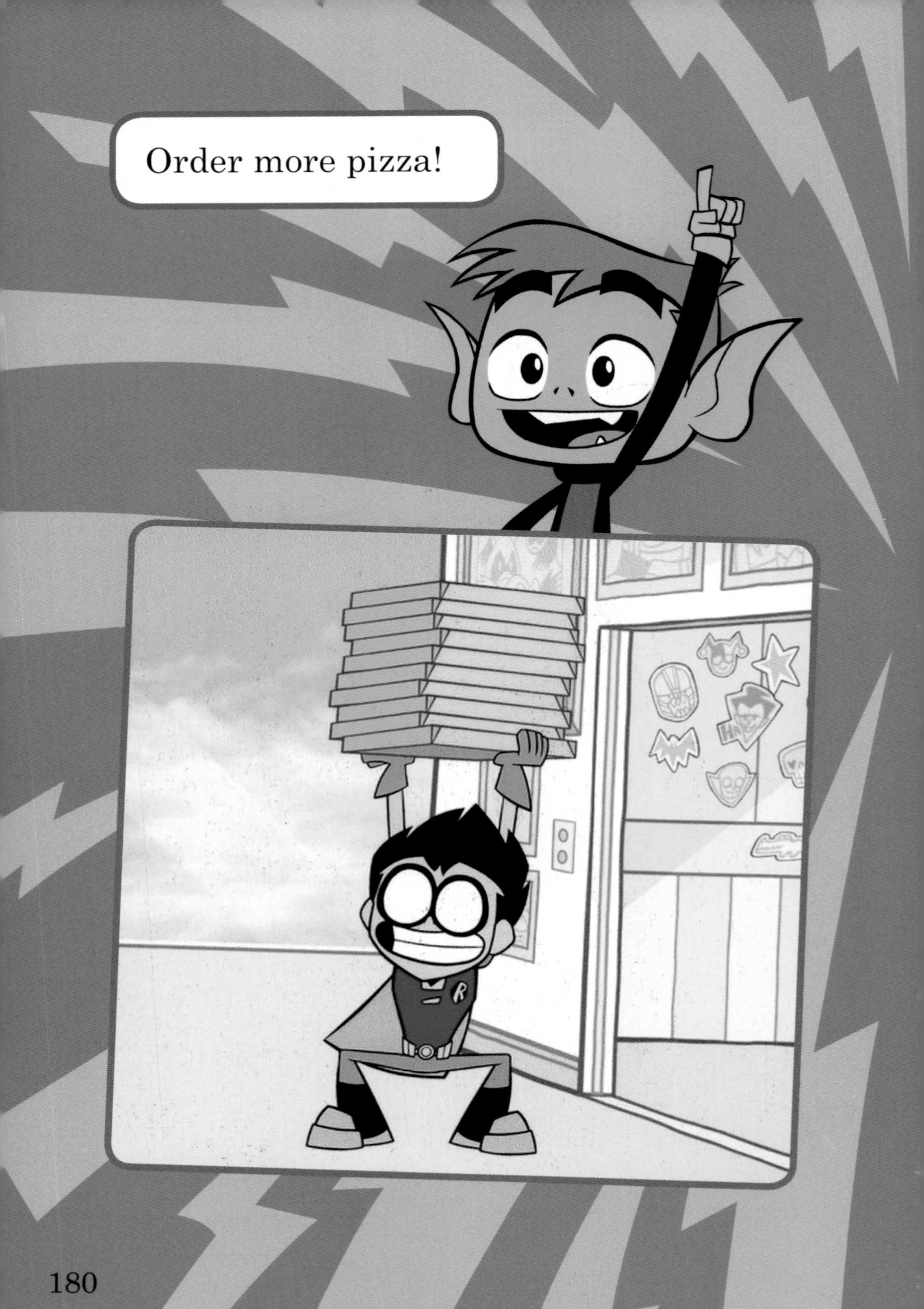
Order more pizza!

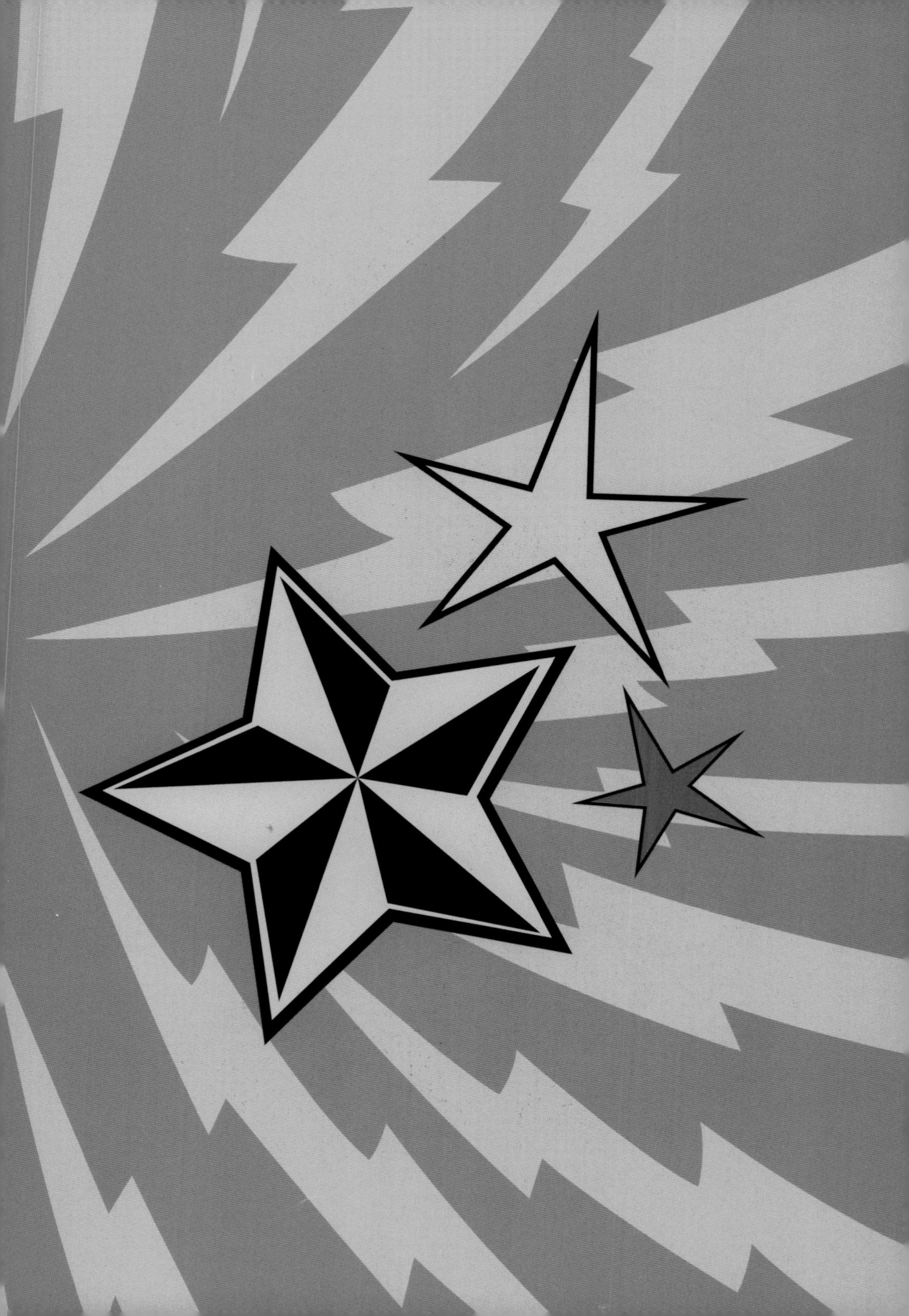

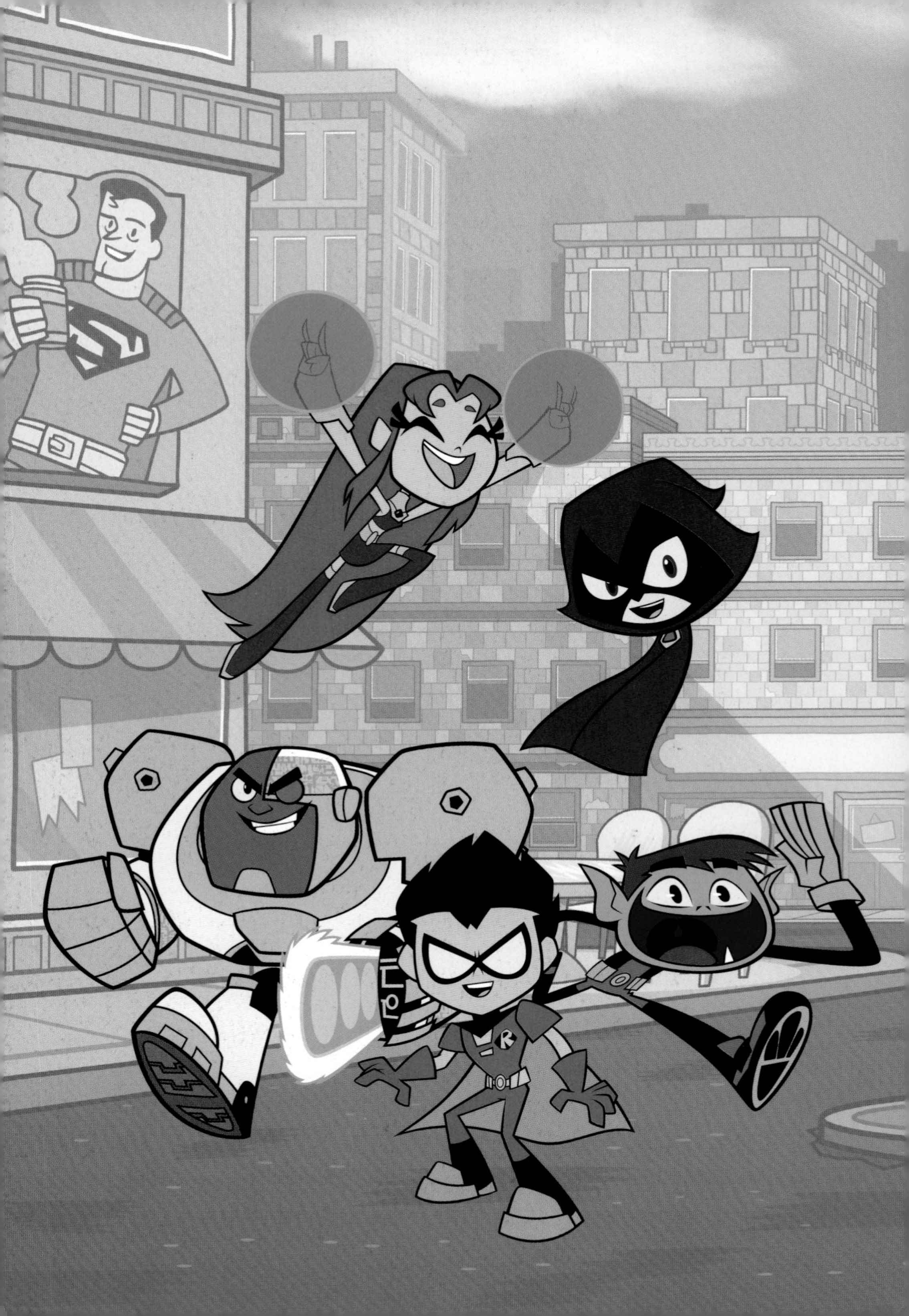

DON'T MISS:

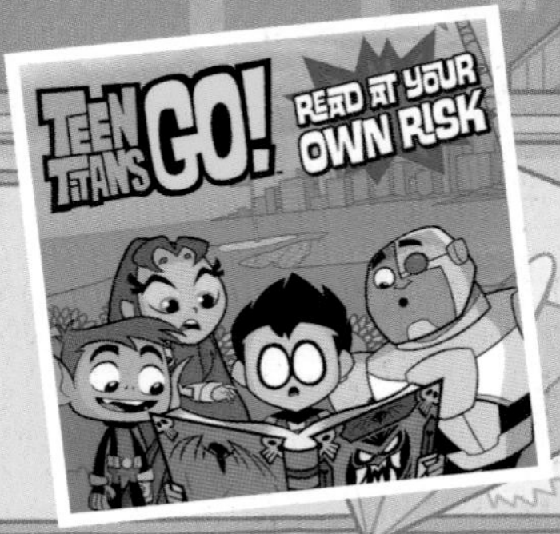
TEEN TITANS GO!
READ AT YOUR OWN RISK

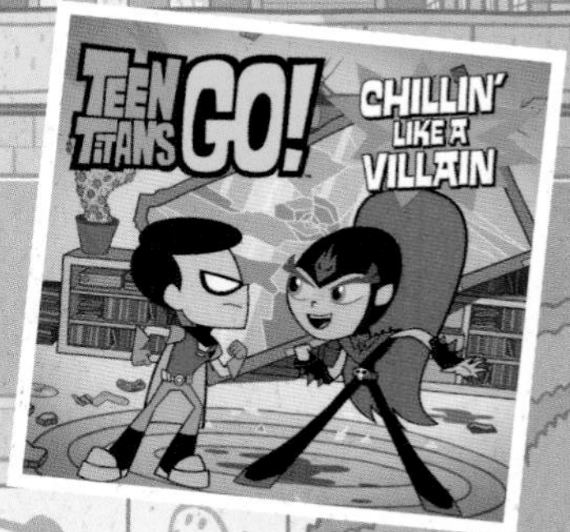
TEEN TITANS GO!
CHILLIN' LIKE A VILLAIN

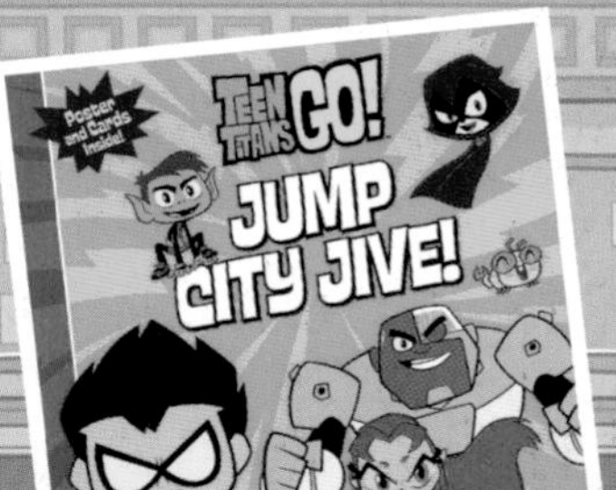
Poster and Cards Inside!
TEEN TITANS GO!
JUMP CITY JIVE!

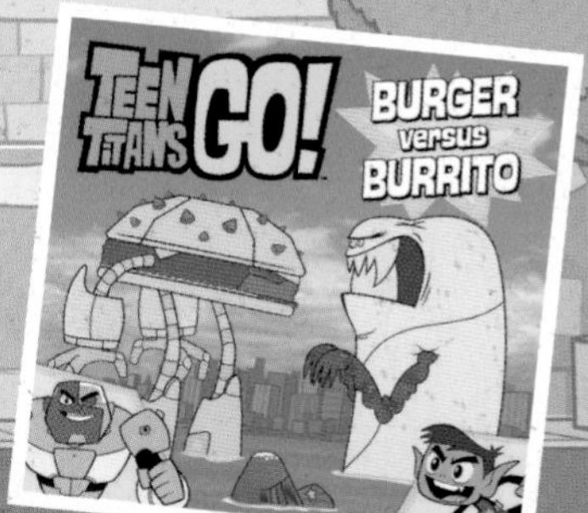
TEEN TITANS GO!
BURGER versus BURRITO

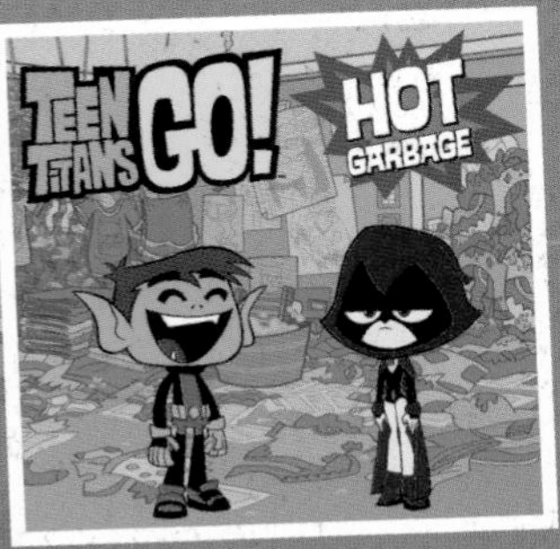
TEEN TITANS GO!
HOT GARBAGE

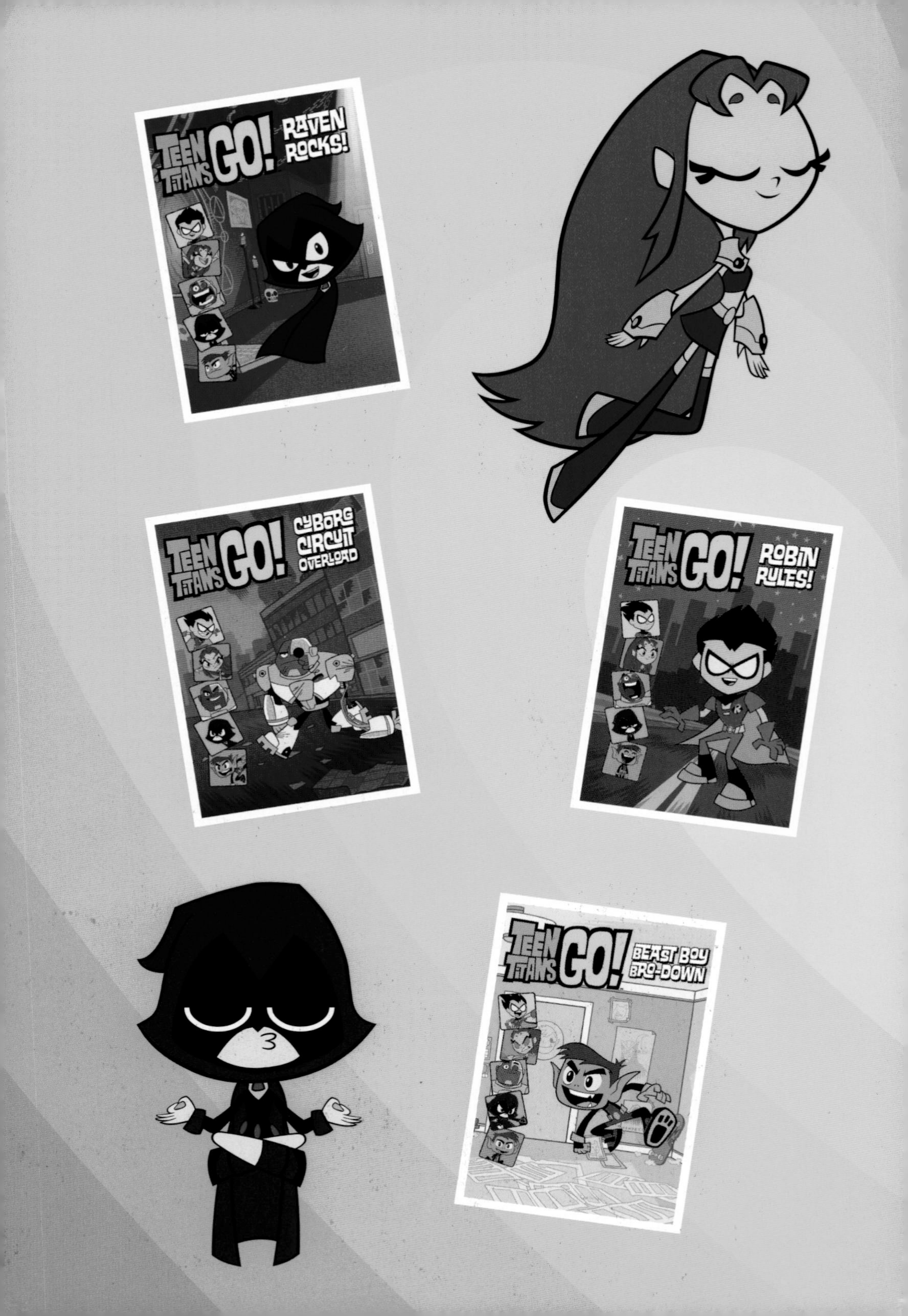
TEEN TITANS GO!
RAVEN ROCKS!
TEEN TITANS GO!
CYBORG CIRCUIT OVERLOAD
TEEN TITANS GO!
ROBIN RULES!
TEEN TITANS GO!
BEAST BOY BRO-DOWN

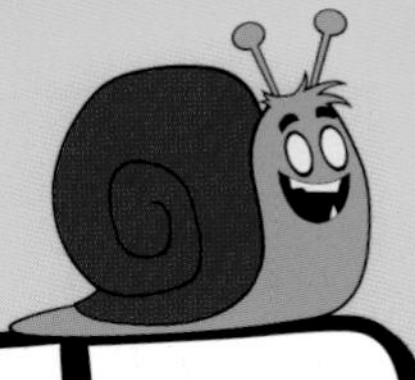

READ THESE NEXT!

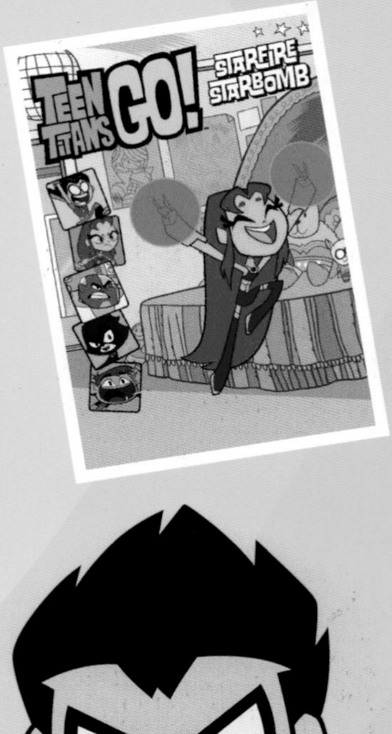
TEEN TITANS GO!
STARFIRE STARBOMB

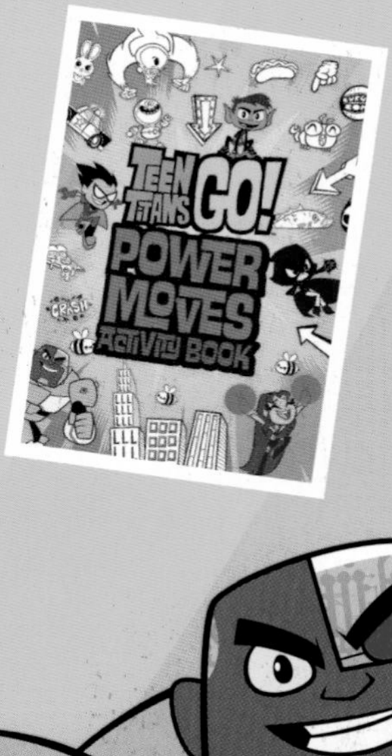
TEEN TITANS GO!
POWER MOVES
ACTIVITY BOOK

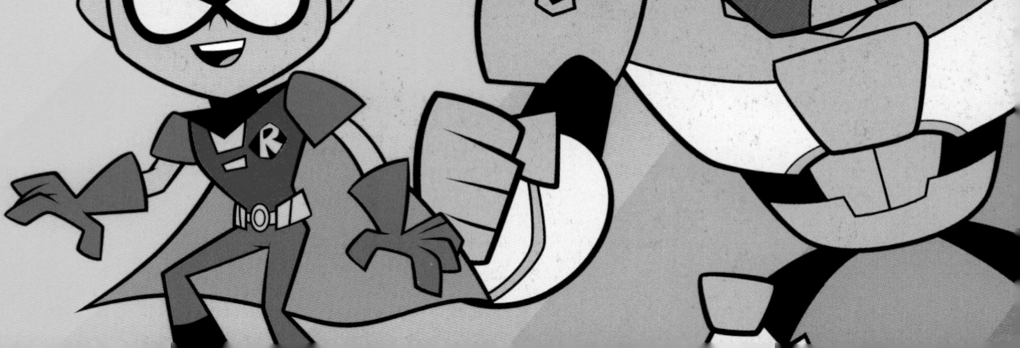

CHECKPOINTS IN THIS BOOK ✔

Teen Titans Go!:
Meet the Teen Titans

WORD COUNT	GUIDED READING LEVEL	NUMBER OF DOLCH SIGHT WORDS
545	L	94

Teen Titans Go!:
Boys Versus Girls

WORD COUNT	GUIDED READING LEVEL	NUMBER OF DOLCH SIGHT WORDS
304	I	60

Teens Titans Go!:
Tooth Fairy Freak Out

WORD COUNT	GUIDED READING LEVEL	NUMBER OF DOLCH SIGHT WORDS
362	H	66

Teen Titans Go!:
Brain Food

WORD COUNT	GUIDED READING LEVEL	NUMBER OF DOLCH SIGHT WORDS
279	I	59

Teen Titans Go!:
Silkie Time

WORD COUNT	GUIDED READING LEVEL	NUMBER OF DOLCH SIGHT WORDS
279	I	62

Teen Titans Go!
Pizza Power

WORD COUNT	GUIDED READING LEVEL	NUMBER OF DOLCH SIGHT WORDS
186	I	49